THE PHANTOM SURFER

With their Starhurst School friends, Jean and Louise Dana spend spring vacation at Horizon, located on the Atlantic coast. The seaside resort town is being restored to its former Victorian-era character. But the restoration project is plagued by thievery and sabotage.

The Danas and their favorite dates, Chris Barton and Ken Scott, are plunged into the thick of the mystery when they witness a lumber theft, discover that signals are being sent from an abandoned lighthouse, and see the nocturnal surfer who time after time mysteriously vanishes before reaching shore.

In between thrills and spills while learning to surf, the lively teen-age detectives face many hazards in their attempts to trap the plotters responsible for the sabotaging of the restoration project.

The railing cracked loose and Louise pitched forward

The *Dana Girls* Mystery Stories

THE
PHANTOM
SURFER

By Carolyn Keene

GROSSET & DUNLAP
A National General Company
Publishers   *New York*

PRINTED IN THE UNITED STATES OF AMERICA

CONTENTS

CHAPTER		PAGE
I	Runaway Horses	1
II	Disastrous Lesson	10
III	Surfing Sisters	18
IV	The Sleepy Constable	26
V	A Hard Trek	34
VI	Threatening Notes	43
VII	Haunted Lighthouse	53
VIII	Well-kept Secret	61
IX	Wiped Out!	70
X	Black Water	80
XI	Puzzling Signal	88
XII	Strange Villagers	96
XIII	Flying Feet	105
XIV	Spyglass View	116
XV	Sneaking Figures	124
XVI	Police Surprise	132
XVII	Eavesdropper!	141
XVIII	An Accusation	151
XIX	Planning an Attack	160
XX	Pirates' Passageway	169

THE
PHANTOM SURFER

CHAPTER I

Runaway Horses

"A phantom surfer? You're kidding!"

The exclamation had come from Doris Harland who was in the Dana girls' dormitory room watching them pack.

"I'm not kidding," replied blond-haired Jean Dana. "I got it straight from Mrs. Osborne." The sixteen-year-old girl's blue eyes sparkled with excitement.

Her dark-haired sister Louise said, "And her husband backed her up. When they went to Horizon after exam period to make arrangements for our spring house party, they heard the story from an old fisherman."

Doris was eager to learn more. "And what else did Mrs. Osborne tell you?" she asked Louise, who was a year older than Jean and more serious.

Jean grinned as her sister replied, "The phantom

surfer appears only at night. He comes toward shore and disappears."

"Sounds like a real phantom all right."

Louise said that the Osbornes had also told her another interesting fact about Horizon. It had been a thriving Victorian seaside resort but gradually was abandoned. Recently, former summer residents and others interested in restoring the community had put up money for the project. Very little had been accomplished, however, because of continued thievery and sabotage.

"Can't they do anything about it?" Doris asked. The pretty, brown-haired girl was one of the Danas' closest friends at Starhurst School.

"Apparently not," Louise answered. "I guess the twenty-five inhabitants of Horizon don't care enough about the project."

"Or are just plain discouraged," Doris commented. She stood up and moved toward the door. "I'd better go look over my own clothes for the trip." She giggled. "My entire wardrobe will be blue, because that's Charlie's favorite color. And we should please our dates."

The house party was to consist of girls from the junior and senior classes whose recent grades were high. Each girl could invite a boy she especially liked and the group would be chaperoned by young Mr. and Mrs. Osborne, who were teachers at Starhurst.

Louise and Jean were leaving a day early because they planned to stop at their home in Oak Falls before going on to Horizon. Since the death of their parents, the girls had lived with their maiden aunt, Harriet, and her bachelor brother, Captain Dana, of the transatlantic liner *Balaska*. Uncle Ned could not get home often and his nieces always made a point of trying to see him whenever he flew from New York to Oak Falls.

As Doris was about to leave, another close friend of the girls, Evelyn Starr, walked in.

"Guess what?" the slender, dark-haired girl asked. "Lettie Briggs is furious at you, Louise, and vows she's going to get even for keeping her out of the house party."

"Me?" Louise said. "Lettie is always furious about something and playing mean tricks. But how in the world can she blame me because she can't go?"

Evelyn chuckled. "You remember your A plus in Mr. Osborne's geology course?"

Louise nodded.

"Well," Evelyn went on, "you probably don't know this. Mr. Osborne has a different marking system from most of the other teachers. He scales everyone's grades according to the highest mark in the class. So your A plus ruined Lettie. She barely squeaked through."

Jean burst out laughing. "Lettie sure can be far out sometimes. Louise, I guess you needn't worry about her getting even with you for a while. She won't have a chance until we get back to school."

In the rush of packing and attending last-minute classes, the Danas forgot about Lettie. When she passed them in the hall that night, they thought they detected a smirk on her face. Was she scheming something already?

The slender, cross-looking girl roomed with Ina Mason, and while Ina was pleasant when not in Lettie's company, she seemed to be under the girl's spell most of the time.

The following morning the school bus came to take the Danas to the airport. Just before they climbed aboard, Doris came running from the building. There were tears in her eyes.

"What's the matter?" Louise asked quickly.

"I just had a phone call," Doris gulped. "Charlie can't come to the house party."

"But you talked to him last night and everything was all right," Jean remarked. "Why can't he go?"

"He has measles!" Doris burst out. "Now of course I can't go either."

Louise and Jean looked at each other, then Louise put an arm around the sobbing girl. "You're coming, anyway. Now don't say No."

"Oh, Louise, I couldn't do that. You all have dates and I'd be a fifth wheel."

"That's silly," Jean spoke up. "Louise, Ken, Chris, and I would love to have you join us. You worked hard for your good marks and you've earned the trip. You must come."

Doris smiled. "You're too good to me, but I'll meet you in Horizon if you say so. You'd better hurry now or you'll miss your plane." She hugged her chums good-by. "See you in the South!"

Louise and Jean hurried off and a few hours later were greeted at the Oak Falls Airport by Aunt Harriet and Uncle Ned. Miss Dana embraced her nieces tightly while her brother looked on.

Then he said, "My turn. Ahoy, my hearties!" This was a favorite expression of the tall, robust sea captain.

"Ahoy, yourself!" Jean said as she kissed him.

"It's so good to see you both again," Louise put in.

When they reached home, the front door was opened by the young woman who had worked for the Danas for several years. Her name was Cora Appel. Mischievous Jean could not resist the temptation of reversing the name to Applecore, and the maid good-naturedly accepted her nickname. Unfortunately she was inclined to be clumsy and hardly a day went by without a minor accident in the house.

"Applecore!" Jean exclaimed and hugged the girl as the Danas entered the front hall.

"Let me have your bags," Cora said at once. "I'll take them upstairs."

Poor Cora had gone up only five steps when she stumbled over one of the suitcases. It slipped from her hands and bumped down the steps.

"I've done it again!" she said, her voice trembling. "I just can't seem to do nuthin' right."

"Why, that's not true," Louise consoled her. "I'll help you. These bags are too heavy for one person."

She picked up the suitcase and followed Cora up the stairs. The rest of the day was spent in an exchange of news, and bedtime arrived much too soon.

The next morning the four Danas returned to the airport. Uncle Ned had to fly back to New York City. Louise and Jean boarded a plane for Lawrenceville, a small town two miles from Horizon.

When they reached Lawrenceville, the girls were surprised to learn that the only public conveyance to the seaside resort was an old-fashioned carryall. The elderly driver said his name was Royster.

"Climb in, girls," he said. "Hope you ain't in a hurry 'cause Molly and Sadie—that's my team—are gettin' along in years like me and don't like to go fast any more."

Louise and Jean grinned. "We're on vacation," Louise said, "so I guess it doesn't matter."

The carryall had gone barely a mile when Royster became quiet and the Danas discovered he had fallen asleep. At first the horses paid no attention to his dozing. They seemed to know their way to Horizon.

Molly and Sadie suddenly reared, however, giving the carryall a hard jerk. A rabbit crossing the road had spooked them. The lines were yanked from Royster's hands and he tumbled out onto the sandy shoulder of the road.

The next moment the horses dashed wildly up the road. For a few seconds Louise and Jean clung to the handrails of the carryall as it swayed from side to side.

Then Jean cried out, "We must stop the horses!" She started climbing to the front seat.

Louise followed, hoping they could reach the lines. But they found this was impossible. The leather straps had slid down to the animals' hind hooves. There was only one way to stop Molly and Sadie—climb onto their backs and yank hard on the reins.

The move was a dangerous one, but the girls were accustomed to riding horses and managed to climb forward without being thrown off. They grabbed the lines and in a few seconds had Molly and Sadie under control. When the horses finally halted, Louise and Jean curled the lines firmly about their hands and dismounted, then climbed up to the front seat. Louise took the four lines. She wrapped the two on the left around the others, and guided the team with the lines on the right.

After turning the carryall around, she drove back to Royster.

"Are you hurt?" Louise asked the white-haired man, who was sitting up and rubbing the back of his neck.

"Guess not," he replied. "Jest a little dizzy, ma'am." He started to get to his feet but teetered shakily.

Jean jumped down to help him. "You'd better get into the back seat and take it easy," she said. He was more than willing to accept her suggestion.

"You young ladies are mighty brave, I'll say," Royster complimented them. "Molly, Sadie, you behave yerselves now."

The horses cocked their heads as if to nod Yes and whinnied. Louise snapped the lines gently against their chestnut rumps and drove the rest of the way. Royster directed her to a side road, a short cut that skirted town. It led directly to a section of the shore where the Horizon Inn was located. The two-story hotel was an attractive building with a wide veranda and a large lobby.

"Um," said Jean, "a real groovy place."

The girls went at once to the desk and identified themselves. Mr. Smith, the clerk on duty, looked surprised to see them.

"You girls canceled your reservation," he said. "I've given your room away."

"We must stop the horses!" Jean cried out

CHAPTER II

Disastrous Lesson

"Louise! Jean!"

Starhurst students and their dates converged upon the Danas. Among them were two athletic-looking boys, Ken Scott, tall, slender, and blond. His friend Chris Barton was slightly shorter and dark-haired. Ken, somewhat reserved, was Louise's special friend. Chris, considered a comic by his friends, had come at Jean's invitation.

"Are you all right?" Ken asked. "The driver of the carryall told us his horses ran away and he fell out and you girls had to bring the team under control."

"We're okay," Jean replied. Then she grinned. "You should have seen us riding old Molly and Sadie bareback. Real circus performers."

Though all the listeners felt that the incident had been dangerous rather than funny, they laughed at Jean's humorous description. It was nearly five minutes before the Danas could repeat what the desk clerk had just told them. Their friends were astounded.

"You never canceled your reservation," Doris said stoutly.

"Of course we didn't," Louise replied, "but Mr. Smith says we did."

Jean turned to the desk clerk. "How did you get word of a cancellation?"

The flustered man turned around and reached into a pigeonhole which adjoined the section for keys and letters. He brought out a telegram sent from Penfield where Starhurst School was located. In amazement Louise and Jean read:

MY SISTER AND I UNABLE TO COME. CANCEL
RESERVATION. LOUISE DANA

"If you didn't send it, who did?" the clerk asked.

The Danas said they did not know, but since Mr. Smith had given away their room, they would take another.

"But I have none left," he told them.

"Well, Louise," said Jean, grinning, "I guess you and I will have to sleep on the beach."

Doris spoke up. "Mr. Smith, have you assigned Charlie Romer's bed to anyone else?"

The clerk consulted his room list. "No, I haven't," he replied.

"Then," Doris went on, "perhaps his roommate could bunk with some other boys and Louise and Jean could have that room."

Chris seconded the idea. "Sure, he can move into our place. We'll put in a cot. I'll sleep on it."

The boy in question attended the same school as Ken and Chris. They went off to look for their classmate and found him on the beach. He said he would be very glad to give up his room to the Danas.

"That's great," said Louise.

Mr. Smith smiled. "I'm relieved too. If you young ladies will just make yourselves comfortable for half an hour or so, I'll have the transfer made and get the room ready for you at once."

Meanwhile, their friends put on swimsuits and went out on the beach. Louise and Jean left their suitcases at the hotel desk and decided to walk around the inn and get acquainted with its layout. There was an indoor and an outdoor palm garden where dancing was held nightly. The beach was very wide, and although the sand reached to the porch steps, the girls were told that the water never came higher than halfway up the slight slope.

"It's a beautiful place," Louise remarked. "We ought to have a marvelous vacation."

The Danas walked around to the back of the inn where the carryall had brought them. A shiny chauffeur-driven limousine was just pulling up.

Louise and Jean glanced at the occupants, then groaned.

"I don't believe it!" Jean exclaimed. "Lettie Briggs!"

"And Ina Mason and Mrs. Briggs."

Jean giggled. "And two handsome boys. How in the world did Lettie manage to snare them?"

Louise was thinking fast. Lettie had blamed her for not being able to join the Starhurst house party. Maybe this was how she was getting even. Louise knew there were bound to be some unpleasant incidents between them in the next few days.

Suddenly Jean turned to Louise. "I'll bet a cookie Lettie sent that telegram!"

Louise was inclined to agree. Who else would have any motive for doing such a thing?

"I think you should go up right now and accuse her," Jean declared.

Louise shook her head. "If Lettie did do it," she said, "and then finds out you and I have a room anyway, she'll be more furious than ever. Let's go!"

The Danas hurried off to the beach. It was a beehive of activity. Some of their friends had set up a volleyball match with several other house-party groups also staying at the inn. The orange and white beach ball bounced quickly from hand to hand. Other guests were stretched out on the beach enjoying the sun and watching the game. Many were swimming and a few surfing.

As Louise and Jean reached their Starhurst friends, they spotted two familiar heads bobbing above shimmering waves some distance from shore.

"Ken! Chris!" the sisters called out.

The boys waved, then in a flash took long strokes toward shore. In a few moments they were out of the water, toweling themselves and talking excitedly about Horizon and its wonderful beach.

Attention soon focused on one young man. He was tall, deeply suntanned, and had rusty-blond hair. From the way he rode the waves on his surfboard it was evident he was an expert.

"Who is he?" Louise asked.

"A surfing instructor," Evelyn replied. "Mr. and Mrs. Osborne have engaged him to give our group lessons. We're lucky, because some of the other house parties had already signed him up."

Louise watched intently as his graceful figure caught each wave just right and rode in on a board tilted about halfway up the side of the rolling water. At times he would come to the nose of his surfboard and curl all his toes over the front of it.

"That's called hanging ten," Ken told her.

On another ride to the beach, the surfer stood two-thirds of the way back on his board, with its nose tipped upward.

Finally Jean asked in amazement, "Doesn't he ever fall off?"

A boy from one of the other house-party groups who was standing nearby replied, "I haven't seen Bing Master fall off yet."

Presently the surfer came out of the water carrying his board, which he laid on the beach alongside several other boards. After surveying the crowd a few minutes, Bing walked directly toward the Starhurst group. At once Mr. Osborne stood up and greeted him.

"I want you to meet the members of our house party," he said.

The surfer acknowledged the introductions, then sat down to chat. He learned that just a few of the boys and girls had ever been on boards and only while lying flat; none of them had ever tried standing up and riding in.

"It's a fascinating sport," Bing told them. "Some people literally live for it. They go on 'surfaris.'" The handsome young man smiled infectiously. "I hope that by the time you all go home you'll be expert surfers."

The Starhurst visitors laughed but each one doubted that this could happen. The Danas mentioned the marvelous feats of their future instructor. During the lively conversation, they learned that Bing was twenty-four, had not been out of college long, and was teaching surfboard riding as an interim "fun" job.

Suddenly he looked all around the group, then asked, "Is any girl here without a date?"

Doris shyly admitted that she was.

"Then," said Bing, "you have just acquired a partner. How about going to the dance with me tonight?"

Doris blushed. "I'd love it."

Louise, Jean, and Evelyn exchanged glances. They were very happy about their schoolmate's sudden luck.

"Maybe we should start getting acquainted," Bing told Doris. "How about lesson number one for you in the surf right now?"

Doris looked a little frightened. "You mean on a board?"

"Yes. Don't worry. We'll go together. All you'll have to do is stand still. I'll take a large foamie and guide it in."

"All right," Doris said. "I don't want to get my hair wet. I'll run up to my room and put on a cap."

After she had gone, Jean turned to Bing. She asked, "Have you ever seen the phantom surfer?"

The young man frowned and looked at her searchingly. Finally he said, "Surely you don't believe that story."

With a grin Chris spoke up. "Sure she does, and she's going to catch him!"

Bing smiled but made no comment.

When Doris returned, the others watched as Bing picked up a large foam plastic board and led her into the water. He did not go very far out and the ride in on the waves was a perfect one. Those on shore clapped loudly.

Encouraged, Doris agreed to a second ride. This time Bing took her out into deeper water. During a calm he helped his partner onto the foamie, then swinging up himself, he gave her a few tips on surfing.

"This time crouch a little," he directed.

As the board began to whiz toward shore, Doris panicked. She suddenly turned and grabbed Bing. The next instant both of them wiped out under the wave. Bing reappeared almost instantly, grasping the surfboard.

Doris was nowhere in sight!

CHAPTER III

Surfing Sisters

THE girls on the beach screamed and the boys began shouting to Bing. He seemed to be having a hard time locating Doris.

"Oh, maybe the board hit her and knocked her out!" Evelyn wailed.

Surfers nearby rushed to the spot where Doris had gone down. Within seconds after the wipeout, Bing and another swimmer had dived under the crashing surf. To everyone's relief, they dragged up the gasping girl and carried her to the beach.

Louise and Jean ran to the spot. "Oh, Doris, are you all right?" Louise asked.

Her friend, pale and a bit shaky, answered wanly, "Before we t-took off for shore, Bing told me if ever I felt I was going to fall off—" Doris broke off in a coughing spell, then went on speaking in gulps. "H-he told me to take a deep breath, relax, and fall seaward. I tried my best but I was terrified.

When I fell off the board, I stepped in a deep hole and couldn't get out. Bing rescued me just in time. I couldn't have held out two more seconds."

The other girls insisted that Doris lie down and rest. Seeing that Bing looked worried about her, Doris said, "It was my own fault. You told me to hold the crouching position, but I didn't follow your instructions."

He smiled at her. "I didn't think lesson number one was going to be over so soon. I'm sure you won't psych out the next time."

The lure of the water was too much for the Danas. Feeling certain that their room would be ready by this time, they went to the inn and put on swimsuits. As soon as they returned to the beach, the two girls joined their dates for a refreshing swim. They noticed that Bing had erected a red flag near the vicinity of the hole, warning everyone to avoid the area.

When Louise and Jean emerged from the surf for a rest, Bing came over to talk to them. He had just finished instructing a couple of boys.

"How about you Danas taking a lesson?" he asked.

"I'd like to," Louise answered.

"Then you come first," he said. "I'll be back for you in a little while, Jean."

Louise waded into the water with the instructor. Bing carried his surfboard on his head safari style.

Then he sailed it in front of him as they swam out beyond the breakers.

"All set?" he asked.

"I'm ready."

They climbed onto the board, with Louise in front of Bing. As they rode toward shore, Louise found she was balancing herself and not depending entirely on Bing to maneuver the board.

"We'll just follow the line of the wave," he said.

It all seemed so easy, but Louise knew it took hours and hours of practice to learn how to balance one's self on the board in rough water.

"Inch your left foot forward," Bing instructed his pupil. Louise slid her foot along the deck, then held this position until they arrived in shallow water.

"Oh, that was fun!" she exclaimed. "Thanks a million."

"You're an apt student," Bing praised Louise. "You seem to have a real knack for cutting the waves. Tomorrow you'll have to try riding in on a board yourself."

He walked toward Jean, who was already rising from the sand. "Would you think me too bold," she said, "if I try riding alone?"

Bing laughed. "I see you're adventurous." He turned around and gazed at the water, then said, "I think it will be all right. I'll ride near you. Just remember that if you feel yourself wiping out—

that's falling off—try hard to hang onto your board so it won't hit you."

"I'll remember," Jean promised.

Keeping about twenty-five feet apart, they swam out, then hoisted themselves up onto the boards.

It was an ideal ocean for a beginning surfer. The water was reasonably calm and the waves seemed to be following a set pattern. Jean found that she had no trouble in shifting her weight from side to side, bending over, straightening up, catching the waves. While she was still in deep water, Jean caught sight of Lettie Briggs not far from her.

Lettie was lying face down on a small board and using her feet as propellers. Before Jean realized what was happening, the spiteful girl had pulled directly in front of her.

To avoid a crash, Jean was forced to sway to the left, going headfirst through the waves and losing her surfboard. Fortunately it did not hit her.

When Jean came to the surface, her eyes were blazing. By this time Lettie was nearing the beach and Jean set out with fast strokes after her.

"Why did you do that?" she demanded.

"I've got a right to do anything I want to," Lettie replied flippantly. "I'm not with your group."

Jean set her jaw and stared straight at Lettie. "I've had enough of your mean tricks," she said.

"What do you mean—mean tricks?" Lettie parroted. "I couldn't help it that I crossed in front of you."

"I don't believe that," said Jean, "and furthermore it was pretty low-down of you to send a telegram signed with Louise's name."

Lettie lowered her eyelids but said, "I don't know what you're talking about."

"I think you do," Jean retorted. "You get pleasure out of such strange things, I just don't understand you."

"I don't care whether you do or not," Lettie answered. "I'm having a wonderful time here and no thanks to you or your sister." She walked off down the beach.

By this time Bing had retrieved Jean's board and brought it to shore.

Lettie rushed up to the young instructor. "Oh, Bing," she said in her most honeyed tones, "you're so cool and simply terrific in the water. You must give me lessons. I don't care what it costs."

The young man looked at her in disgust. "I charge everyone the same price," he said. "But I have no time left to give you lessons. Several weeks ago I was engaged by some house-party groups. My schedule is completely filled."

Lettie showed her annoyance. "I'll see to it that you change your mind," she said and marched away.

Louise and Jean had heard the conversation and broad smiles spread across their faces. When Bing came over, he said, "Where does that girl go to school?" Upon learning that Lettie attended the same one Louise, Jean, and Doris did, he looked surprised. "I don't see how you get along with her."

"We don't," said Louise, "but at times Lettie makes life exciting for us."

In a little while everyone returned to the inn to dress for dinner. Tables for eight had been set up in the main dining room. The Danas, Doris, Evelyn, and their dates were able to be together.

As a special welcome to the newcomers, a unique selection of dinners had been arranged by the Horizon management. Luscious pastries, decorated with colorful sugar crystals, completed the menu. As an added surprise for her table, Louise had cut out tiny paper surfers and requested they be set at each place.

Picking up her favor, Jean said, "These are cute, Louise," and added, "I think I almost like surfing better than mystery-ing!"

The conversation continued to be light-hearted during the delicious meal. All of them declared they had "eaten much too much."

The weather had turned very warm, and although the dancing was outdoors, the young people felt uncomfortable. The afternoon breeze had completely disappeared and the air was very still. There was bright moonlight and the couples were content to sit on the beach rather than dance.

About ten-thirty Ken said that he would like to take a walk. "How about looking around the town of Horizon?"

Louise agreed to go. "I'm game, but I understand it's a sleepy place. Probably nothing will be open and nobody up."

Jean and Chris said they would like to go, but the other couples preferred a walk on the beach. Before leaving, Louise sought out Mr. and Mrs. Osborne and explained their plan.

"Is it all right with you?" Louise asked Mrs. Osborne.

"Yes. Go ahead, but don't stay out late," she replied, smiling.

Her husband laughed. "I'd say there won't be enough excitement in that village to keep anyone more than ten minutes."

The two couples set off. As they approached the town, Jean remarked, "This sure is a spooky place. Every house is dark."

The moonlight was bright and the occupied buildings and those being restored stood out in clear silhouette.

Suddenly Jean grabbed Chris's arm. "I heard a noise!" she said. "Listen!"

The four young people stood still. They were near a church which was being rebuilt. To one side of it stood a lumber truck almost filled with boards.

Now the Danas and their dates could hear the

murmur of voices. A couple of sentences came to them clearly. "We got enough. We'd better leave some so nobody will get suspicious."

A moment later two men jumped into the cab of the truck and started the motor. Then it backed toward the street.

Louise whispered to the others, "Those men are stealing that lumber!"

CHAPTER IV

The Sleepy Constable

As the Danas and their dates stood wondering what to do about the possible theft of lumber, they heard the driver say, "Listen, Mike. There's not a soul around this dead old town. Why don't we stop up the street and take those plumbing tools from the schoolhouse?"

"Sure, Mack," the other man agreed. He laughed. "No worries anyhow. We got plenty of protection."

The truck pulled up the street. At once Chris said to his companions, "Are we just going to stand here and let them get away?"

"No sir!" Ken replied. "You and I ought to be able to take those men by surprise."

Quickly Louise spoke up. "Don't do that. They may be armed. I think we should report them to the constable and let him take over."

"I agree," Jean said.

"Do you know where he lives?" Chris asked.

The girls had to admit they did not know. However, considering the meager population of Horizon, it should not be difficult to find him.

"But we must hurry," Jean urged.

The two couples set off in the direction opposite to that taken by the truck. They passed one dark house after another. Then luck favored them. They saw a dim light in a small white bungalow with a picket fence around the front yard. The foursome hurried up the rickety porch steps. Jean pressed a button alongside the screen door.

"Oh, somebody please come," she mumbled anxiously.

Shortly a freckle-faced little girl in a short summer bathrobe lifted an inside latch. Jean judged her to be about four or five years old. "Yes?" she asked with a yawn and opened the porch door, pressing her nose against the screen.

"We're looking for the constable," Louise spoke up quickly. "Do you know where he lives, dear?"

"Nope," the child answered, shaking her mop of red curls.

Thinking that perhaps the sleepy-eyed child did not know what the word "constable" meant, Chris said confidently, "He's the man in charge of all policemen around here."

"Yeah? I don't know where his house is. Mommy and Daddy aren't home and Gramp's asleep. Can't wake 'im up. Be madder'n a hornet."

The visitors chuckled at the little girl's grown-up manner.

"Do you have a telephone?" Jean put in.

When the little girl nodded, Louise said, "May we come in to look through your phone book? It would take only a minute and we'd love you for it."

"I'm not supposed to let strangers in," the child replied, starting to close the door.

"Oh, wait a minute. Please," Jean begged. "We saw some bad men trying to steal lumber up by the church."

"And we've got to report them right away," Ken put in urgently.

The plump-faced child bit her lip, then relented. "Oh, okay. You can come in. But be very quiet."

She led the group into the living room and introduced herself as Babs. "Wait here. I'll bring the phone book to you."

Louise and Jean looked about the quaintly decorated room—hooked rugs and embroidered chair seats and family portraits in heavy gold frames.

The boys were much too agitated over the evening's events to be intrigued by decor. "You women! How can you be so calm?" Chris said nervously.

Ken chuckled. "A couple of pros! That's why

they get so many cases to solve without developing a case of nerves, old boy!"

Louise and Jean were about to comment, when Babs reappeared and handed them a crumpled directory. Jean flipped through it until she found the list of special town departments.

"Here it is!" Jean sighed in relief.

As she noted the constable's name and address, her sister turned to Babs. "Honey, can you tell us how to get to Winding Way?"

The child pointed her chubby fingers toward the front door. "That's our street."

"Thanks a lot," Chris cut in and grabbed Jean's hand. Ken took Louise's, and before the girls could protest, rushed them outside.

"Just a second, Chris Barton." Jean halted him. "First, which way do we go?"

As the couples turned about to see the number of Babs's home and her neighbor's, Jean cried out, "*The constable lives next door!*" She pointed to a lamppost on which two numbers were painted, then repeated the listing she had seen in the phone book:

Constable John Ritter
35 Winding Way

"What!" her friends said in astonishment. "But why didn't Babs—?"

"Well, let's not stand here theorizing," Chris broke in. "We've wasted enough time!"

They rushed up to the front door and twirled

the old-fashioned bell handle. It rang loudly but no one came to answer it. They tried again, then began pounding on the door.

Finally they heard a second-floor window fly up. A man leaned out. Jean almost giggled at his appearance. All she could think of was the poem *The Night Before Christmas*. The constable wore an old-fashioned, long-sleeved nightshirt. A red nightcap covered his hair completely.

"Who is it? What do you want?" he called down in an annoyed voice. Before anyone could tell him, he eyed the couples speculatively and said, "I ain't a justice o' the peace. If you folks want to get married you can't in Horizon. My advice to you is forget it and go home."

The four young people burst into laughter.

Louise said, "That's not what we came for. We want to report a robbery."

"A robbery?" the man exclaimed in amazement. "You mean here in Horizon?"

"Yes."

"Well," he said, "I'm not the one for you to come to."

"Aren't you the constable?" Ken asked.

"I'm only the daytime constable," was the surprising answer.

"Then who's the nighttime constable?" Chris demanded.

Ritter leaned both elbows on the window sill and rested his chin on his hands. "To tell you the truth we ain't got one. There's no need. Nobody's goin' to come to this place to take anything, 'cause there ain't nuthin' to take. I s'pose you're stayin' at the inn with all those young people. Well, go on back there and let me get back to bed. You got a nerve wakin' me up."

Louise reiterated why they had come. "Lumber is being stolen and also plumbers' supplies. If you can't take care of it, how about calling the State Police?"

"All right. I'll do that." He slammed down the window.

The young people walked away, each doubting that the sleepy constable would bother to telephone the police.

"Let's go to that schoolhouse and see what's going on," Jean proposed.

By the time they reached the building, the truck was just backing out and getting ready to leave. There was no owner's name on either side of it. They memorized the license number. If the men were not picked up by the State Police, the Danas could at least report the number.

Suddenly Jean whispered, "Why don't we climb aboard and see where the truck's going?"

"Good idea, Sis," Louise agreed. "I can't think of a better way to follow Mike and Mack!"

"If you say so," Ken agreed along with Chris.

Quietly they pulled themselves up onto the pile of lumber. The truck rumbled away. It was not easy to hold on. The road was bumpy and the driver sped along.

Louise said to herself, "This was not such a good idea after all. It's dangerous."

The truck took the short cut leading out of Horizon toward Lawrenceville. The vehicle went on and on. Once they passed a lighted house and the young people were tempted to jump off but the truck's speed was now too great. Also, they were afraid to move for fear the load of lumber might suddenly shift.

"We shouldn't have done this," Ken whispered to Chris. "The first chance we get we ought to climb off."

"Maybe the men will stop for some reason—perhaps to unload," Louise tried to console her friends.

"Then we may be in a worse situation," Ken declared. "I doubt that we could explain our way out of this one."

"Don't despair, friend," said Chris. "We can always say we were touring Horizon, spotted their truck and decided to improvise a hayride!"

The others chuckled quietly. In a pinch perhaps they could plead their case as four mischievous teen-agers out for an evening of fun.

At the moment the truck showed no sign of stopping or even slowing down. As they rode in silence, the Danas began to wonder about Constable Ritter. Such indifference to thievery only a few blocks from his home was inexcusable. Was he just sleepy and lazy? Or was there more to it?

"We've heard about the slowdown in restoring the old buildings," Louise thought. "Is it possible that the constable is winking at the thefts?"

Jean had been thinking along the same lines. "Maybe Ritter gets a cut of what is stolen and sold."

The two girls were rudely shocked out of their reveries. The speeding truck had come to a crossroads. Now the driver made a sharp left turn. As a result, the whole load of lumber suddenly shifted to the right. The vehicle was likely to turn over!

"Jump to the other side!" Ken cried out. "Into the sand!"

CHAPTER V

A Hard Trek

LIKE four giant grasshoppers the Danas and their escorts leaped into the air. They cleared the truck and landed with thuds in a sandy grass field.

They had made their escape just in time. The great pile of lumber slid with a roar to the opposite side of the vehicle.

The driver was evidently in a panic. He swung the vehicle from side to side as he gradually put on the brakes. Apparently he knew enough not to stop short for fear of having the boards crash through the cab. But one by one the rattling planks began to slide off the vehicle and landed behind it on the road.

By now the truck had ceased wavering and came to a stop a moment later. Would the men emerge to check the load? Would they spot the couples who had pitched themselves into the field?

Fortunately the truck started up again and with a burst of speed pulled ahead.

"Is everyone all right?" Louise queried the others.

"Topside up," Ken replied.

Jean and Chris reported that they were all right but Jean complained that she had not enjoyed landing feet first with high-heeled shoes. She kicked them off.

"Here go mine too," said Louise. Her toes felt cramped and a bit bruised.

"Well, where do we go next?" Jean asked. "We've lost the truck, we're miles from the beach, and no transportation."

"Suppose I hike back to the inn and borrow a car to pick you all up," Ken said.

Louise had been surveying the landscape and the sky. The moon had moved a bit since they had left the inn. At that time it had hung directly in front of the building. She figured it could still keep them on course, should they decide to walk back without using the road.

"When we left the inn," she said, "the moon was shining into the lobby. Now it's straight ahead of us across the grass and dunes. I'm sure this field would be a short cut."

Ken smiled. "I see what you're driving at. If we go across the dunes, we ought to pretty nearly hit home base."

Chris figured they could make it in half the time it would take going by road. "Who wants to try it?"

All the others were game, but Ken asked the girls what they planned to do about their shoes.

"I think it'll be easier going if I take my trek in bare feet," Jean replied.

"I will too," said Louise. "But before we go, shouldn't we clear the roadway a bit? These planks are dangerous for drivers."

"You mean lift all this lumber to one side?" Jean asked.

Louise nodded. The others agreed and the work started. Suddenly Jean burst into laughter. "This is the first time I ever worked on a thief's job."

"You're behind boards instead of bars!" Chris told her.

The work had barely started when the young people heard a car coming. As it rounded a bend in the road, they saw the revolving, flashing light on the roof and realized it was a State Police sedan. They waved their hands and the driver stopped. There were two officers in the car.

"What's going on here?" the driver asked. He surveyed the couples' soiled clothes and added, "Where'd all these boards come from?"

Ken started to explain, then said, "Maybe we ought to introduce ourselves first."

The four quickly told their names and Jean

"What's going on here?" the state trooper asked

asked, "Did Constable Ritter phone you about the lumber thieves?"

"We got no such message," the officer replied. "What's this about thieves?"

Louise described the conversation she and her friends had overheard between Mack and Mike and how the foursome had reported the theft of lumber and plumbers' supplies to John Ritter.

"Then we attempted to trail the men ourselves," she concluded.

The trooper asked which direction the truck had taken. She told him and also gave its license number.

"There wasn't any name on the truck," Jean added.

"I'm not surprised," the trooper said. "Thieves usually are pretty cautious. No doubt they painted out the name so they couldn't be traced."

"What about the license plate?" Jean queried. "Do you think they stole that too?"

"I suspect so," was the reply.

Before the officers pulled away, the driver used his radiotelephone to alert headquarters.

The other policeman spoke up. "You say Ritter knows about all this. I realize he's a crochety fellow, but he should have gotten in touch with us immediately."

The group also thought Constable Ritter's behavior peculiar, almost suspicious, but decided not to say so. They declined the policemen's offer of a ride back to the inn and urged the officers to try locating the truck.

"You kids are really on the ball," the driver said, smiling. "I appreciate your getting these boards out of the way. We'll arrange to have them returned to the church and tell the builders what happened."

The police car zoomed off and soon its lights were swallowed up by the darkness.

"That sure was luck, having the troopers come along," Chris remarked as he and Ken picked up another plank.

"It's too bad we didn't get a look at Mack and Mike," Louise said, "but at least we can identify them by their voices."

As soon as all the lumber had been moved off the road onto the adjoining field, the couples started across the uneven ground in the direction of the moon. At first the walking was fairly easy since the terrain was completely sandy with hillocks of long grass around which the trekkers could step.

In a little while they came to a series of sand dunes and here the walking was arduous. They climbed up one dune and down another. Presently the girls began to lag behind and admitted that their feet hurt.

"I know it's silly, but I'm going to try it with my shoes on," Jean told her sister.

She sat down a moment and adjusted them, then climbed up the next dune. As she started down the far side, one ankle turned. Her shoe came off and she lost her balance. Jean went head over heels down the dune!

"Oh!" cried Louise from the top.

She made her way to the bottom as fast as she could. Her outcry had alerted the boys, who were some distance ahead. They turned and rushed back.

"What happened?" Chris asked.

Jean, seated in a heap, smiled ruefully. "High heels and sand dunes don't go together," she said, and told of her tumble.

"Would you like a piggyback ride to the inn?" Chris asked.

"I'll be all right in a few minutes. We ought to rest, anyhow."

They all sat down and discussed the evening's events. Had the troopers caught the lumber thieves? What were Mack's and Mike's full names? Were they members of a gang or just small-time thieving partners?

Finally Jean declared she was ready to go on and they started off again. As they reached the summit of the next dune, which was a particularly high one, Louise suddenly exclaimed, "Why, there's a lighthouse!"

It stood at the end of a rocky promontory, clearly silhouetted in the moonlight.

"I know where we are," Ken spoke up. "You remember the beach curves outward a little way from our hotel? Well, beyond that there's an indentation in the shoreline and this promontory juts out from it."

They all gazed at the old building. Its tall, slender base rose up gracefully to an iron-railed balcony which completely surrounded the tower.

"According to the desk clerk, the lighthouse isn't used any more," Ken told the others. "Probably it has been left standing for sightseers."

Louise had been gazing intently at the building. Suddenly she cried out, "Look! Someone's flashing a light from the top!"

Within seconds the light went out. As the onlookers watched, they noticed a side door in the base of the tower. A few minutes later it opened from the inside and a man stepped out. He disappeared behind the building.

"I wonder what that was all about," Louise mused.

No one could answer her query and the four young people started off again. This time the dunes carried them down to a wide, empty stretch of beach.

"Isn't the moon gorgeous?" Jean said.

"And those waves are super," Ken added. "Wouldn't it be fun to get a surfboard and try a little riding?"

"At night?" Louise exclaimed.

"Why not? It'd be fun!" he declared. He had

hardly said this when their attention was drawn to a particularly high wave. Were their eyes playing tricks or was someone riding on its curl? The figure coming through the spray was clothed in pure white and looked like a statue carved from marble.

"It's the phantom surfer!" Jean cried out.

CHAPTER VI

Threatening Notes

THE watching group stared unbelievingly. So the story about the phantom surfer was true!

The ghostlike figure expertly dipped and rose as he neared the shore. Suddenly he disappeared under a gigantic curling wave and did not reappear.

"He must have been caught in a tube or a pipeline," Chris remarked.

"A pipeline?" Jean queried.

"That's a long hollow space created when the wave forms a perfect arch and leaves a corridor of air underneath it," he explained.

The amazed onlookers waited for the phantom to reappear. They watched for ten minutes but did not see him.

"If that was a man instead of a ghost," Louise remarked, "he probably drowned."

Ken reminded her that according to the local

story, the phantom had repeated this act many times. Ken grinned. "He's a real specter!"

The couples started up the beach for the inn. When they reached it, Jean heaved a sigh of relief. "Boy, am I glad to be here!" She looked down at her bedraggled clothes and swollen feet. "Tootsies," she said, "into the tub you go!"

"Mine too," Louise remarked.

The sisters said good night to the boys, adding that they would see them at breakfast. The girls slept soundly, but as soon as Louise was awake the next morning she picked up the room telephone.

"Operator," she told the woman at the switchboard, "please give me State Police Headquarters."

"Oh," the woman said, "do you need police help?"

"No," Louise answered. "I just want to inquire about something."

She was connected with the barracks but hesitated to mention details of the previous night's episode. Louise had a hunch that the operator was listening. If the woman spread the story, the news of the lumber theft might become grossly exaggerated. Furthermore, the Danas' part in the adventure would be revealed. Nevertheless, curiosity overcame Louise and she inquired if the thieves had been caught.

"No, Miss Dana," said the officer at the other end of the line. "The men got away and abandoned the truck. They had stolen it as well as the license plates. At the moment we have no clues, and if you can offer any further information, we'd appreciate having it."

"If I think of anything else, I'll let you know," Louise promised. She thanked the officer and hung up.

As soon as breakfast was over, the sisters went to their room to change into swimsuits. Both wanted to resume their lessons in surfing.

When they reached their room, Hilda the chambermaid was busy making the beds. "Good morning," she said, then walked over and closed the door. "I just heard that you girls are detectives," she added in a whisper.

"Where did you hear that?" Jean asked.

Hilda hesitated a moment, then said, "I guess it wouldn't do any harm to tell you. I got it from the telephone operator." The Danas were not surprised to learn this.

"Oh, we like to delve into mysteries and try to solve them," Louise said.

Hilda walked up to the girls and looked at them intently. "I need your help and so do the other chambermaids here."

"What do you mean?" Jean asked.

Hilda explained that she and the rest of the girls had come from Lawrenceville to Horizon Inn for the spring and summer seasons.

"We like it here and we want to stay, but we're scared to."

"Scared?" Louise asked. "What about?"

"We all got threatening letters!"

"Who sent them?" Jean questioned the chambermaid.

"They weren't signed. But they said if we didn't leave here, we'd all be harmed," she told them. "Oh, what'll we do? Some of us are depending on these jobs for extra spending money during the school year."

"Have you talked to Mr. Olney, the owner?" Louise queried.

"No. To tell the truth, we've all been too afraid to do anything."

Louise and Jean were silent for so long that Hilda said, "Aren't you going to help us?"

Jean nodded. "Of course we will. But has it occurred to you that perhaps these letters were sent as a practical joke?"

"Oh, no, I'm sure they weren't," Hilda replied.

Louise asked to see one of the letters. The chambermaid hurried off but returned within five minutes.

"Here it is," she said, handing over the envelope.

Louise frowned. "This was not sent in the mail. How did you and the other girls receive yours?"

Hilda explained that the letters had been left at the desk while Mr. Smith was off duty. Louise opened the envelope and took out the note. It was typewritten on plain paper with no heading and no date. As Hilda had said, it was a warning for the recipient to leave the employ of the Horizon Inn at once or risk harm.

"Jean," said Louise, "I don't think this is a joke." She handed it to her sister.

After Jean had read it, she agreed.

"What do you advise us to do?" Hilda asked. "We really do need the money and it's too late now to find other jobs."

Jean asked her if she or the other chambermaids knew of any suspect. "Maybe someone who has a grudge against Mr. Olney."

"Oh, I'm sure no one could be so cruel," the girl answered. "Mr. Olney is very nice and I can't believe he has any enemies."

Louise and Jean said they would be glad to do some investigating and try to find out where the letters had come from and the motive behind the vicious threat.

"Will you and the other chambermaids be willing to remain until we can find out something?" Jean asked.

"I will. And when I tell the others about you, I know they'll stay on for a while longer," Hilda replied. "Thanks an awful lot."

Louise and Jean went downstairs again and told the desk clerk that they would like to see Mr. Olney.

"I'm sorry, but he's busy right now," Mr. Smith told them.

The Danas said they would wait. The owner's

office door was open and it was soon evident who his caller was, even though she was out of sight.

Lettie Briggs was complaining in a loud and unpleasant voice that her mother's room, Ina's and her room, and that of their dates had not been attended to. "We demand that you do something at once," she said sharply.

"I'm very sorry, Miss Briggs," Mr. Olney replied. "Your rooms will be taken care of as quickly as I can arrange matters. Unfortunately a couple of our chambermaids left last night. The one assigned to your rooms happens to be among them."

"That's no excuse," Lettie told him. "I want you to know I have traveled a great deal and I know how a hotel should be run."

Louise and Jean looked at each other and then at Mr. Smith. Grins spread over their faces and Jean had to restrain herself from laughing out loud.

Lettie went on haughtily, "My mother and I will expect everything to be taken care of within the next half hour."

"I'm sorry, but I can't promise that," Mr. Olney replied. His quick answer indicated to the Danas that his temper was growing short.

Lettie's reply was startling. "My father's a very influential man," she told the inn owner. "He could ruin your business if he wanted to."

Apparently this was too much for Mr. Olney. In a clipped voice he said, "If your father is a successful businessman, I am sure he would know that one does not attain success through unreasonableness. Now if you will excuse me, Miss Briggs, I have work to do."

Lettie flounced out of the office. As she came around the corner of the lobby desk, she almost bumped into the Danas. The irate girl glared at the sisters, annoyed and embarrassed that they had heard the interview and her dismissal.

"So you've been eavesdropping," she said to them.

Jean could not resist a gibe. "Lettie," she said, "if you don't like it here, why don't you send Mr. Olney a telegram canceling your reservation?"

The unpleasant girl flung her chin into the air and hurried off. Mr. Smith, still grinning, went to tell Mr. Olney that the Danas would like to speak to him. By the time they walked into his office, the owner had regained his normally good-natured disposition.

"Good morning," he said. "Can I be of assistance?"

Louise explained what Hilda the chambermaid told her. "Have you seen any of the notes which have been distributed to your employees?" she asked.

"No," he answered, puzzled. "Notes about what?"

Louise placed Hilda's warning note in front of him. He read it quickly and frowned.

"I had no inkling of this, but it explains why two

of my chambermaids left yesterday. As a matter of fact, they didn't even give a reason for quitting and I just figured something had come up to call them home."

The hotel owner was greatly disturbed and thanked the Danas for bringing the note to his attention. "I am in a rather difficult position to try persuading the girls to remain. I'll be in touch with the police, but I'd appreciate your assistance. Would you two mind helping?"

Louise told him of their conversation with Hilda and assured him, "We'll do all we can and let you know how we make out."

The Danas returned to their room, where Hilda was eagerly awaiting them.

"More trouble!" she said. "Now my cousin Helen and the entire staff of waitresses have received letters like mine. The girls all say they're going to quit."

"Oh, that would be terrible!" Jean exclaimed.

"We must try to stop them!" Louise urged. "Hilda, will you go with us to the girls' rooms so we can talk to them?"

The trio hurried off to another building where the whole second floor was used as a huge dormitory. They found the large group chattering excitedly and packing suitcases.

"Oh, how can I get their attention?" Hilda asked. "I'm afraid what you Danas want to do is hopeless." As she spoke, tears began to roll down her cheeks.

Louise, however, would not accept defeat. She found a tumbler and tapped a spoon on it loudly. Within seconds there was silence.

"I'm Louise Dana, one of the guests here," she said. "Hilda has shown me her copy of the threatening letter. If only one of you had received the warning, it might be considered more serious. You know as well as I do that nobody can harm all of you at once. I'm sure if you stick together, the person who sent the warning will not dare carry out the threats."

Jean introduced herself and said she and her sister had promised Mr. Olney they would try to solve the mystery. He, of course, would be in touch with the local police.

"It's just possible that some spiteful person is trying to play a joke on Mr. Olney. I admit it's a very mean one. Out of fairness to him and to yourselves, don't you think you should reconsider before leaving here? Your work is pleasant, and as Hilda told us, it is late in the season for you to try getting other jobs."

The waitresses and chambermaids looked at one another. Finally a girl called out, "It is kind of a mean thing to do to Mr. Olney. He has been very nice to us. What say we stick it out a little longer? Maybe we won't get any more warnings with the Danas on our team."

Louise asked, "Is that agreeable to everyone?"

One by one the various girls nodded. The Danas were breathing sighs of relief when the telephone near them rang. A waitress named Amy took the call.

"Hello," she said. "Whom do you wish to speak to?"

Suddenly her face turned deathly pale. She let the phone drop from her hand and slumped on a nearby bed in a faint.

"Oh!" several girls screamed.

Jean instantly jumped to the telephone and said, "Would you mind repeating that?"

A man's gruff voice replied, "All of you girls quit at once or your families will be harmed!"

CHAPTER VII

Haunted Lighthouse

THE caller who had given the dire warning hung up abruptly.

"Who was it? What was the message?" Louise asked her sister quickly.

Jean repeated it in a low whisper, out of hearing of the rest of the girls.

In the meantime, several of Amy's friends were trying to bring her back to consciousness. They were rubbing the back of her neck and chafing her wrists. Hilda had gone for a towel wrung out in cold water and now put it on Amy's forehead. In a few seconds Amy opened her eyes and looked around, puzzled at the anxious faces.

"What happened to me?" she asked.

"You fainted," Hilda told her. "Did it have something to do with the telephone call?"

The question brought an immediate reaction

from Amy. She sat up and a look of terror came into her eyes.

"It was a man! I don't know who he was. He said—he said that if all of us girls don't leave here at once, harm would come to our families!"

Her listeners gasped. One of them asked, "Are you sure you heard him right?"

"I'm positive!"

Jean stepped forward. "He said the same thing to me."

At once the dormitory broke into a frenzy. Girls cried out. Some began to weep, and others went to work furiously to finish packing their suitcases. The Danas' pleas were ignored.

Hilda came up to Louise and Jean. "This settles it!" she said. "You had me persuaded to stay, but now I must think of my family's welfare before that of Mr. Olney or the Horizon Inn. I'm sorry."

Louise and Jean went from girl to girl, coaxing and pleading that they ignore the warning and continue working. Their effort was in vain, though, except for two chambermaids and two waitresses. All of them were older than the other girls and had no immediate families to worry about.

"But we can't serve everybody in the inn," one of them declared.

"Of course you can't," Louise agreed. After a moment's thought, she added, "I have an idea. Practically all the guests in the inn are of high school age and quite used to serving meals and keeping their rooms tidy."

Jean grinned. "All but Lettie Briggs," she said under her breath. Aloud she told the maids who were staying that she was sure the Starhurst and other house-party groups would be glad to help out in the emergency.

"What's most important is to find out who the man on the telephone was and who wrote the threatening letters."

Regretfully she and Louise said good-by to the girls who were leaving and went back to their own room.

Louise remarked, "Whoever the troublemakers are, I am sure they're involved in the mystery of Horizon and the sabotage and thefts. Someone is doing his best to get rid of the regular people around this place and discourage visitors from coming."

"Yes," Jean said. "I suppose we ought to tell Mr. Olney we failed in our mission. Guess it'll be some consolation, though, for him to know we and our friends will pinch-hit as waitresses and chambermaids until he can hire replacements."

They hurried downstairs and told the owner the bad news. He was greatly disturbed and said he would drive into town immediately and insist that the constable put out a warrant for the malicious man.

"I'm afraid you won't find Mr. Ritter very cooperative," Louise spoke up. "Anyway, do I have your permission to ask all the house-party girls if they would help out?"

"I would be most grateful," Mr. Olney replied. "Please tell them that I will correct the situation as soon as possible."

The Danas found everyone willing to cooperate except Lettie and Ina.

"The whole thing is perfectly ridiculous!" Lettie exclaimed. "Mr. Olney is the worst hotel manager I've ever met. And if he thinks I'm going to be my own waitress, he has another guess coming!"

Jean was furious. "For Pete's sake, Lettie, why don't you go home? You're just a big pain around this place!"

Lettie flung her head into the air and retorted, "Well, I'll tell *you* something. If you want to be a servant instead of a high-class paying guest, you can do it." She walked off in a huff.

Louise shook her head. "That girl is hopeless."

Jean smiled. "Louise, I have a prediction to make."

"What is it?"

"I'd like to bet," said Jean, "that those attractive young men Lettie and Ina invited here won't be able to stand either of them much longer. It wouldn't surprise me if their dates walked out on them."

Once more the Danas went to Mr. Olney's office. He was delighted to hear of the cooperation of his young guests, except two. With a resigned smirk he said, "I'll assign one of the chambermaids who is staying to the Briggs' rooms."

"I have a suggestion to make," Louise said.

"Yes?"

"Instead of service at each dining table, suppose you set up a long table with all the food on it and let each guest help himself buffet style? Then later we girls will carry the dishes to the kitchen."

The inn owner beamed and said it was a fine idea. He would inform the cooks and put the operation in motion.

"My chefs will like this," he added. "As a matter of fact, they have complained of not having a greater part in showing off their skills. They'd love to put on their big hats and serve in the dining room."

"Wonderful!" Jean exclaimed. "I think it would be more fun than being waited on at the table."

The Danas went back to their room and put on swimsuits, beach slippers, and robes. A few minutes later they met Ken and Chris on the beach. To their surprise no one was in the water.

"It's cold," Ken explained. "And the wind is making the surf too treacherous to go in. How about a fast game of volleyball?"

The match proved to be a lively one, but soon the beach became crowded and they had to give up the game. They stretched out on the sand, but in a short time found that it was too chilly for comfort. The sky was overcast with thick rain clouds.

"How about a walk?" Ken suggested. "That's a good way to keep warm." He buttoned his beach coat tightly.

"Any suggestions which way?" Chris asked.

Louise answered. "How about the lighthouse? I'd like to see what it looks like inside."

"Hope it isn't locked," said Jean.

The four young people set off and in a short time reached the old landmark. With the bleak sky and dune sands whipping about it, the building did not look so romantic as it had in the moonlight. The Danas and their companions walked out onto the rocky promontory and circled the lighthouse. Its entrance door was on the south side and had no lock on it. Ken pushed it open wide enough for them to look in. At once a mournful wailing sound came to their ears.

"What's that?" Chris asked.

The wailing continued at an even pitch.

"Maybe it's only the wind," Ken suggested.

Louise and Jean were skeptical that it was the wind. When the wailing stopped, they could still hear the roar of the wind.

"I think it's just another piece of the Horizon puzzle," Louise said. "It was supposed to scare us away from here."

Chris grinned. "A haunted lighthouse, eh? Kind of early for spooks to be out!"

Ken added in a whisper, "Perhaps the phantom surfer lives here!"

"Let's find him," Jean proposed. "Maybe he's up in the tower."

Ken insisted upon leading the way up the circular iron stairway, with Chris bringing up the rear. He reminded the others of the light they had seen in the tower.

"If we do find anyone, he may not be friendly and I wouldn't want you girls to be harmed."

When the young detectives reached the top, they found the room empty. The great light that had once flashed warnings to ships was gone now and no one was in sight.

"Let's go out on the balcony," Louise proposed. "There should be a wonderful view from up here."

They opened the small door and went outside. As their eyes scanned the ocean, Louise exclaimed, "I see a ship out there but it isn't moving!"

The four watched the small yacht tossing in the rough sea.

"I wonder if it's disabled," said Ken.

As they watched, the reason for its position became evident. A rowboat with a single occupant was trying desperately to make its way across the heaving waves toward the yacht.

"Boy, he's really taking his life in his hands!" Chris remarked.

The small boat finally reached the ship. A ladder was flung over the side and the man made his way topside. Then the rowboat was hauled to the deck.

"If that fellow was planning to hitch a ride, he sure did it the hard way," Jean said. "I'd prefer landing from a copter."

"But maybe he wasn't planning to hitch a ride. He might have been caught in the rough water," Ken suggested. "Let's not get carried away with all this mystery stuff."

Within seconds the yacht got under way. The young people were leaning on the ancient metal rail which surrounded the balcony of the lighthouse. Suddenly the section in front of Louise gave way and she pitched forward!

CHAPTER VIII

Well-kept Secret

As the railing cracked loose between two posts, Ken and Chris made a grab for Louise. Each managed to get hold of an ankle with one hand. With the other they grasped another section of rail which they hoped would stay intact. The wind was blowing fiercely and it was a struggle to keep themselves from falling. To pull Louise back up seemed impossible.

For a couple of seconds Jean had been too terrified to move. Now she jumped forward to help rescue Louise. Lying flat on the balcony, she grabbed both her sister's legs, then began inching her way backward.

Louise tried to reach up and grasp the edge of the balcony but her attempt was in vain. She would have to depend entirely on her rescuers.

Finally, with the combined efforts of her sister

and the boys, Louise was dragged to safety. She tried to stand up but her knees gave way and she sank down.

"Oh," she said shakily, "that was the worst fright I ever had in my life!"

Jean sighed. "And I think it's the worst one you ever gave me."

Ken and Chris also sat down. Ken, gazing intently at Louise, said, "For a second I thought I had lost my best girl forever."

Louise blushed and gave him an answering smile, then she said gaily, "Just think what a chance I offered you all to be heroes!" She gazed at the broken railing. "I don't know who's in charge of this lighthouse, but whoever he is he won't thank me for almost ruining his property."

Ken and Chris stood up and tried to bend back the iron bars. They finally succeeded, but felt that the damage should be reported. Ken added, "Since we don't have anything to write with, I should at least tie a warning signal around this weak section."

Jean pulled a red scarf from her coat pocket. When Ken had secured it, he said, "I'll try to find out whom we should report this to."

Conversation turned to the ship and the rowboat which they had been watching. They were suspicious of their connection with the mystery at Horizon.

Finally Jean stood up. "If you feel okay, Sis, we'd better go. Whatever the mystery is, it's well hidden."

"You can say that again," Chris agreed. "But I'll bet you girls will solve it."

Louise and Jean laughed and assured the boys they would keep alert to any developments. They went down to the ground floor. To their surprise, Doris and Bing were just entering the building.

"Louise!" exclaimed Doris. "Are you all right?"

"We saw the accident," Bing added. "What are you all doing here?" he asked sharply.

Louise said they were sightseeing and had been curious about the old lighthouse.

"There's a great view from up top," Ken put in. "Say, who's responsible for its upkeep?"

"I want you to stay away from here," Bing said, ignoring Ken's question. The others were surprised at his severe tone.

"Why?" Jean asked.

"Because this building isn't safe. It's rickety and too dangerous for you to climb around in. You should know that without my telling you. You nearly fell off and killed yourself, Louise."

None of the foursome replied. They followed Doris and Bing from the lighthouse and started up the beach. Louise deliberately steered Ken away from the others, pretending to pick up some sea shells.

"Ken," she said, "I saw what I'm sure was a trap door in the floor of the lighthouse. I wonder where it leads."

"And you want to go back and investigate it despite the warnings," Ken remarked.

"Yes, I do. And also, if that place is so dangerous, why was somebody up in the tower with a light last night?"

Ken looked at Louise for a long moment, convinced that she had more on her mind than she was telling. Finally he said, "You think the actions of the phantom surfer have something to do with the lighthouse."

"Maybe," she answered. "That trap door perhaps leads to a cellar. Probably someone who was in the lighthouse saw us coming and went down there and made the wailing sounds."

Ken grinned. "You girls are so wise you scare me. Who else would have thought of such an explanation?"

Louise did not reply. Pretending to have all the shells she wanted, she and Ken joined the others.

By the time they reached the inn and had changed into street clothes, it was nearly lunch hour. The girls were due in the dining room to start work on the tables and hurried downstairs.

In the kitchen they found another problem confronting the inn. One of the chefs had been taken ill suddenly.

At that moment Mr. Olney met Ken and Chris in the lobby. He told them of his latest bit of bad luck. "I must have a man to help serve," he said.

"I'd be glad to put on a chef's cap and do what I can," Chris offered, his eyes twinkling.

Mr. Olney thanked him.

Chris made his way to the kitchen. When he appeared in the dining room carrying a huge soup tureen, the girls burst into laughter.

Jean knew from the expression on her friend's face that he was up to some kind of nonsense. Chris called out loudly, "Do you want some more laughs?"

The young waitresses stopped setting the tables and answered, "Yes."

Chris stepped from behind the long table. He walked over to a smaller table and picked up three tumblers which had not yet been filled. He threw the first one into the air, then another, and finally the third. Jumping and dodging, he expertly juggled the glasses. There were Oh's and Ah's from the onlookers and several of the girls held their breath each time one of the tumblers started downward.

Encouraged by his attentive audience, Chris moved to the next table, picked up another tumbler, and sent it high into the air. Then, between catching and tossing four pieces of glassware, he snatched up a fifth and added it to his act.

Everyone in the room was astounded and began

to clap loudly. The applause brought the two chefs from the kitchen. At first they looked disapprovingly at their new assistant, but seeing how expert he was as a juggler, they too laughed and began to applaud.

When Chris finally set the tumblers down one by one, Jean called out, "If the guests don't like the service, you can always keep them happy with a juggling performance."

Luckily everything went along smoothly at lunch. All the guests were there except Lettie and her friends. One of the regular waitresses told the Danas they had driven off into the country to have what Miss Briggs had termed "a respectable meal served in a respectable manner."

"Sounds like her," Jean said in disgust.

Before the girls were ready to leave the dining room, Mr. Olney came to thank them. They all assured him they had enjoyed the work and would be glad to continue until their spring vacation ended.

When he finished talking to them, he took Louise and Jean aside. "I went to see the constable but could get no help from him. He is the most indifferent officer of the law I've ever met."

The inn owner went on to say that he had gone to State Police Headquarters and reported the threatening letters and telephone call which had frightened away most of his employees.

"The officers said they would do their best to find the guilty person but had little to go on."

The Danas said they were still determined to solve the whole mystery of Horizon, but the case became more puzzling each day. "Our luck's bound to change," Jean told him.

The young detectives decided to continue their sleuthing that afternoon, since no one was allowed to go swimming or surfing because of the continued high offshore winds. They asked the boys to walk to Horizon with them so they might look over the restoration project by daylight. The town proved to be larger and more interesting than they had anticipated. At one end of the village was an abandoned amusement park.

"Let's go in and see what's been done," Louise proposed.

The four young people viewed the battered merry-go-round, giant slide with the center board missing, and a caved-in dance floor.

"It's kind of sad to see all of this going to waste," Louise remarked. "If I had ever lived here, even in the summertime, I think I'd want to donate toward restoring the place."

The two couples walked on in silence. They had just rounded a fence which circled a Ferris wheel, when they heard men's voices. They stopped short and listened.

One man said, "Now listen to me, Mike. I want you to shut up. It's easy to put things over on that man Uhler, but you don't have to go around bragging about it."

The other man answered, "Don't get so hot under the collar, Mack. You've done a lot of blabbing yourself."

The two couples exchanged glances. *Mack and Mike!*

"Now's our chance to grab them!" Chris said in a whisper.

"But where are they?" Jean asked in a low voice.

The two men had suddenly become silent and it was impossible to determine whether they were inside the enclosure or somewhere else.

Louise suddenly caught sight of them sneaking from behind a nearby booth. She beckoned to her friends and pointed. Together, the young people began to run after the thieves as fast as they could.

Mack and Mike heard the pounding footsteps and turned. Realizing they were being chased, the men, one tall, one short, took to their heels and raced through the maze of concessions and amusement booths.

"We mustn't let them get away!" Jean exclaimed, taking a deep breath.

Ken suggested the group separate into couples in order to keep the thieves in sight. He and Louise hurried down one path, Jean and Chris another, then paused a moment to listen for any sound of the fleeing pair. Silence.

Had the men escaped? Or were they behind one of the numerous booths or crates, hiding, or even lying in wait for their pursuers?

CHAPTER IX

Wiped Out!

APPARENTLY Mack and Mike were well acquainted with the old amusement park. Louise and Jean thought that they probably had been stealing from the place quite regularly. The girls also wondered who Uhler was.

The young people had lost sight of the fugitives. In the maze of paths and buildings, the searchers did not know which way to go. As a result, their quarry had completely escaped them. Finally the two couples stopped running and met.

"Guess we'd better give up," Louise said. "Anyway, we got a look at the men and can give a pretty fair description to the State Police."

"Yes, and they got a close-up of us," Chris murmured, and added, "I'd hate to have them waiting for me in a dark alley."

The four retraced their steps to the entrance

and walked into the village. They met a woman with a large bag of groceries.

"Pardon me," said Jean, "but do you know a Mr. Uhler?"

"Of course I do. He lives right up the street. You folks must be new around here if you haven't heard of him."

"We're visitors at the inn," Jean told her. "What does Mr. Uhler do?"

The woman said he was head of the Horizon restoration project. "Not that I can say he's done much. But then, he's had a lot of bad luck. You know, things have been stolen and materials haven't been delivered and—" She caught herself before finishing the sentence.

Jean prodded her. "And something else?"

"Well, between you and me—but really it's no secret—he don't get no cooperation from the mayor or the constable and that makes it pretty hard."

"I should think it would," said Jean, who managed not to change the expression on her face, but was excited by this bit of information.

The woman, who said she was Mrs. Philip Phipps, pointed out the contractor's house. The young people said good-by and hurried to Uhler's house. His wife answered their ring and told the callers that her husband was taking a nap.

"Please come back later," she requested. "He don't like folks wakin' him."

Louise spoke up. "We have a very important message for him," she said. "It's about a theft in Horizon."

"Well, all right," the woman replied. "Come in then and sit down."

Her husband appeared in a few minutes, his hair uncombed and his feet bare. Mr. Uhler's trousers were hiked high by tight suspenders which he wore over a T-shirt.

"Howdy," he greeted his visitors. "Your names?"

The Danas and their friends told him, then Louise asked if he knew two men named Mack and Mike.

"Sure I know them," he said. "They help on the restoration whenever I have work for them."

"How well do you know them?" Jean inquired.

Mr. Uhler looked at his callers searchingly. "What are you getting at? Why don't you come right out and tell me what's on your minds?"

Ken told what the young people had learned about the two men and the chase in the amusement park. For a fleeting second Uhler looked a bit frightened. Then he laughed and said:

"I'm afraid you've made a big mistake. Those men are honest and certainly wouldn't put anything over on me."

The four callers had other ideas, but realized it would be impossible to convince the contractor.

After Louise had reported the broken rail at the lighthouse and offered to pay for it, the callers rose.

"I'll let you know," Uhler said. "But stay away from there!"

When the young people left the house, Louise suggested they return to the inn.

"I'm certain," said Ken, "there's some sort of collusion among certain people living here. I can't guess what their motive is, but I'm sure it's not an honest one."

"I agree," said Louise. "As soon as we get to the inn, I'm going to phone State Police Headquarters, and give a description of Mack and Mike and Mr. Uhler's reaction. Maybe we're all wrong, but I'd feel better if the police investigate."

The storm which had been brewing broke that evening, so no one could go outdoors. It cleared the atmosphere and the following morning dawned sunny and warm.

"A good day for surfing," Chris remarked when breakfast was over. "Or, as they say here, 'Surf's up!' "

About an hour later several of the Horizon guests had gathered on the beach, ready to take lessons from Bing. When the Starhurst group arrived, he was already giving a talk on the sport.

"Nobody knows how old the technique of surfing is," he said. "Shipwrecked sailors from the

Bounty found people in Tahiti riding surfboards.

"When Captain Cook brought missionaries to the Hawaiian Islands in 1778, they learned that everybody from the King and Queen down to the lowest retainer was a surfer."

Bing laughed. "It's said that the missionaries were shocked because when the surf was up, everybody left his daily task and went to the beach. Farming, fishing, tapa weaving were forgotten."

Jean whispered to Chris, "Maybe they had the right idea!"

Bing now turned to a specific discussion of what his pupils should remember. "It is very important that you have an excellent sense of timing. Study the waves a while before you go in and decide the best way to ride them. We'll have some contests this morning and use the Hawaiian method of judging. The winner is picked on the length of his ride on a big wave."

"Are there other ways of judging?" Louise asked.

"Oh yes," Bing replied. "In Peru the champion is picked by the size of the wave he rides. Australian judges choose the champ based on outstanding surfing ability regardless of the wave."

Bing asked if any of his students knew some typical surfing language. Doris Harland raised her hand. "If you're excited about the sport, you say you're jazzed on surfing."

"Good. Anybody else?" Bing asked.

A hand went up on the other side and a boy answered, "You can be unplugged," he said with a grin. "It means you're riding free and are in top form."

"That's right. You're all two steps ahead of me," Bing replied. "And now for a little practice. Twelve boards are waiting. I've chosen the following to start." He called Ken's name among them. As the youth went forward he yelled out, "I'm fully pumped."

"What in the world does that mean?" Jean asked.

Doris chuckled. "Bing told me it means that you're rarin' to go. You could also say you're completely stoked."

Bing now chose teams for the contest. Ken, Chris, and two boys from another house-party group were chosen to start. They entered the water eagerly, but on the ride in, all were wiped out but Ken. He was declared the winner.

In one of the women's contests, Doris and Jean were picked to ride with a couple of other girls. It ended in a tie between the two friends.

"You'll have to ride it out," Bing told them.

The girls swam to deep water again, then hoisted themselves onto their surfboards. Jean picked a large wave which she was sure would last for many minutes. As she crouched, shifted her weight and started riding goofy-foot with her right foot forward, it occurred to her how exciting all this was. Sun danced on the water around her. The board made a slight hissing sound and the spray crashed into her body like a thousand tiny needles.

Jean felt very confident and was just about to congratulate herself when something went wrong with her timing. She teetered for a moment. Then suddenly the top foam of the wave curled over. She was wiped out!

Falling seaward, she clung to the board desperately and managed to bring it to shore with her. She grinned at Doris, who had had a perfect ride and was declared the winner.

"Congratulations!" said Jean, panting for breath.

Doris smiled. "Don't forget, I've had the advantage of extra lessons from Bing." She winked at him and he acknowledged it with a big grin.

After lunch the Danas and their dates once more put on beach togs, including robes and slippers. But when they reached the beach, all of them declared that they had had enough swimming for one day.

"What I'd like to do," said Louise, "is investigate that old lighthouse again."

With a twinkle in his eye, Ken asked, "Even though Bing told us to stay away from it?"

"Yes. I'm determined to take a look under that trap door."

Jean was wiped out!

"I'm game," Ken responded. "Let's go!"

When the couples were ready to leave the area of Horizon Inn, they looked around for Bing. He was far up the beach in the opposite direction and hopefully would not notice their absence.

Once again inside the lighthouse, Ken and Chris lifted the heavy iron ring of the trap door Louise had spotted on their first visit. They laid it back and gazed downward.

"An iron ladder," Chris announced. Then, with a grin, he said dramatically, "Methinks there is a cellar in those black depths!"

Jean spoke up. "Sh! I hear water sloshing around down there."

"We can't do much investigating," Ken said. "It's too dark in that hole."

Louise smiled, opened her beach bag, and produced a waterproof flashlight.

Ken laughed. "You amaze me, dear detective," he remarked. "Suppose I take the flashlight and go down."

Louise handed it to him and he beamed the light below. Sure enough, the rungs did end in water. Slowly he descended, then suddenly disappeared and only a faint trace of light was visible. The others assumed he was walking through the water.

After a couple of minutes had gone by, Louise called down, "What do you see?"

There was no answer. Suddenly the last ray of light vanished. Another half minute went by.

"Ken!" Louise shouted at the top of her voice. "Where are you?"

Still silence. The other three looked at one another anxiously.

CHAPTER X

Black Water

"I'm going down to see what happened to Ken," Louise declared and put one foot on the top rung of the ladder.

Chris caught her arm. "No, I want you to stay up here," he said. "If anybody goes down, it will be me."

"But something might happen to you too!" Jean exclaimed.

She had noticed a coil of rope lying on one side of the damp floor and suggested that Chris tie one end around him. The girls would hold onto the other as he made his search for Ken. Chris consented and they made two loops to slip over his arms.

"Now we'll be able to pull you up if you run into trouble down there," Jean said. "Maybe the tunnel leads into the ocean. A riptide might have pulled Ken out."

"Oh, I hope you're wrong," Louise said fearfully.

Chris said he thought the rope would hold. But it was old, shredded, and scratched his flesh.

"We won't yank on the rope unless you tell us to," Jean promised as he started down the steps.

The girls watched anxiously as Chris reached the bottom rung of the ladder.

He called up, "It sure is black in here. I'll try swimming through."

Louise and Jean slowly payed out the rope, hoping that Chris would be all right and would find Ken unhurt. They could hear the hollow echo of his voice as he kept calling the other boy's name. Finally he reported:

"Ken's okay. You were right, Jean. The tunnel does lead out to the ocean. Ken's on his way back. He lost the flashlight."

"Oh, I'm glad he's all right," said Louise, relieved.

The two girls stared into the blackness below. After what seemed an interminable length of time, Ken appeared at the foot of the ladder. Slowly he climbed up and the girls assisted him onto the floor.

"Why, Ken, you're hurt!" Louise cried out.

"It's just a scratch," he answered.

"No, it's not. You have a deep gash in your shoulder," she said.

Ken looked at the wound. It now was bleeding

profusely. As Chris reached the others, he too noticed his friend's injury.

"Man, you've really cut yourself!"

Louise dug into her beach bag and brought out a tiny first-aid kit.

"You do think of everything," Ken remarked as he let her apply some antiseptic.

Deftly she drew the open skin together with adhesive tape and then put on a bandage. Ken thanked her for the first-aid treatment.

"But," Louise said, "I'd feel better if we go to town and have a doctor look at your shoulder."

He objected, insisting that her first-aid treatment was all he needed. Jean and Chris agreed with Louise.

"Okay," Ken said finally.

The trap door was replaced and the rope recoiled and laid where it had been found. Then the four started trekking across the dunes to the village of Horizon.

Jean said, "I don't think we should tell anyone of our trip to the lighthouse."

"But how is Ken going to hide his injury?" Chris asked. "From what I know of the people in Horizon, the story will be all over town in no time."

"Do we have to say how it happened?" Jean countered.

"I suppose not," Ken conceded. "I can always say I had a little accident in the water."

Conversation turned to the tunnel. Louise remarked that it probably was used by the phantom surfer.

Chris grinned. "And probably by pirates coming here long ago."

Louise nodded. "And probably," she stated, "by present-day pirates. Oh, how I wish we knew what the mystery of this place is!"

When the young people reached Horizon, they were told that there was no practicing physician in town. The local pharmacist, however, was a retired doctor. The man proved to be very old and feeble. Ken explained he had injured his shoulder and told what Louise had done.

The doctor studied the professional-looking job and commented, "I guess she's had a course in first aid. The young lady did exactly what I would have done. I'll just replace the bandage."

Seeing that the two couples were in bathing attire, he at once assumed that the accident had happened in the ocean. "Surfboard hit you?" he asked.

Apparently the pharmacist did not expect an answer because he immediately launched into a lecture on the hazards of surfboards and amateur riders.

"My advice to all of you is to enjoy yourselves swimming and forget surfing. It's too dangerous. If crazy folks want to drown themselves or get knocked out with a surfboard, let them do it.

Don't you get banged up. You're too young to go through life with some permanent injury."

Louise gave a pretended sigh. "I guess you're right," she said, relieved that the physician had not asked any more questions.

She and the others bought some tubes of sunburn lotion, candy, and chewing gum. Then they thanked the elderly man for his medical opinion and left the pharmacy.

When they reached the inn, Chris's prediction about the story being spread proved to be true. As they walked into the lobby, Doris, Bing, and several others crowded around them. All demanded to know what had happened to Ken.

He grinned. "I got too daring in the water," he said. "It wasn't a surfboard, though, that whacked my shoulder. It was something else. Don't worry. I'll baby my shoulder for a short time and then it'll be as good as new."

That evening Ken begged off from attending the dance. Louise suggested that he retire at once and he made no objection.

"A good night's sleep and I'll be as fit as King Crab in the morning."

Louise was just debating how she herself would spend the evening when the attractive young man who was Lettie's partner came up to her.

"Hello, Louise," said Bill Potter.

"Hi!"

He sat down beside her and expressed his sympathy over Ken's injury. "I thought maybe you wouldn't mind dancing with me. I'd like to talk to you about something."

Louise was a bit surprised. If Lettie Briggs saw her dancing with Bill Potter, the sparks would surely fly!

"Oh, I'd better not," she answered.

Bill smiled. "I know what you mean. Then how about taking a walk on the beach? There's something I simply must ask your advice about."

Curious as to what it might· be, Louise finally consented. Perhaps it would not take long and they could hurry back before Lettie noticed their absence.

As if reading her thoughts, Bill said, "If you're worrying about Lettie, she's upstairs changing her clothes. She always takes forever, so she won't be down for a long time."

Louise smiled and the two walked out of the lobby and down onto the beach. For a few minutes their conversation was general. He spoke of surfing, of the threat to the staff in the hotel, and of the sleepy old town of Horizon.

"Have you solved the mystery yet?" Bill asked.

"Not yet, and there aren't too many days left in our vacation for me to do it."

Suddenly Bill's mood changed. "There are too many to suit me," he said.

"Too many?" Louise asked. "Why? Is something the matter?"

"Well, Louise," Bill said, "I'd like to go home tomorrow. This is what I want to talk to you about. The plain truth is I can't stand Lettie Briggs!"

Louise smiled. This did not surprise her. But she did not want to become involved. "Oh, Lettie is impetuous," she said. "You have to forgive her for lots of things."

Bill shrugged. "I suppose you have to stick up for your schoolmate," he said. "You know, this whole thing was arranged by Mrs. Briggs and she's paying the bill. That's what makes it embarrassing to me. Can you imagine—me, a hired escort!"

Louise hesitated to comment on this. But Bill insisted upon her advice on how he could get out of the situation diplomatically.

Suddenly an idea came to her. "Why don't you find Lettie a substitute partner?"

Bill looked startled. Finally he said, "I wouldn't wish her on my worst enemy!"

Louise realized that they had walked some distance down the beach and now turned to go back. She tried to steer the conversation into more pleasant channels and asked Bill when he had to be back at school.

"Not until next week, worse luck," he replied.

When the two were almost opposite the inn, but walking near the edge of the breaking surf, they heard their names being called. Louise was sure she recognized Lettie's shrill voice.

"Louise! Bill!" the cry was repeated.

The couple turned to look up to the porch of the inn. Yes, Lettie was standing there.

At that instant a towering wave crashed onto the shore. It bowled Louise and Bill over and knocked them with great force to the sand!

CHAPTER XI

Puzzling Signal

In vain Louise and Bill tried to regain their balance. Desperately they clawed the wet sand, rooting their fingers deeply. But the backwash of the tremendous wave swung the struggling couple around and carried them seaward.

"I mustn't panic," Louise told herself.

In a few moments she and Bill recovered their calm. With strong strokes, they managed to stay together and reach the safety of the beach. Exhausted and bedraggled, they stood up and turned to look at the subsiding water and at each other's sopping clothes in disbelief.

Bill laughed nervously. "I didn't suspect that even a little walk with you, Louise, could be so dangerous," he said. "Actually it's the most exciting thing that's happened to me this vacation."

Louise chuckled and looked down at her bare feet. "My shoes must have come off in the water," she said ruefully. "I guess I'll have to offer a reward for them. But here's hoping the fish don't get them first."

Bill was studying a low incoming wave. He waded into it and to Louise's amazement picked up her missing shoes.

"How wonderful!" she cried. "Thanks a million, Bill!"

He took her arm and together they walked across the wet beach toward the inn. Lettie Briggs met them at the point where the sand was dry. Her face was livid.

"Are you two crazy?" she asked. "Going into the surf with your clothes on?" Before Louise and Bill could answer, she went on, "Of course I'd expect anything of Louise Dana. But I didn't think, Bill, that you'd let her entice you into doing such a nutty thing."

"It was an accident," he told her.

"Accident?" she shrieked. "Don't give me that stuff. Louise is just trying to take you away from me. Well, she got her punishment all right. I don't see anything especially pretty about her now. Louise, you look worse than a wet rag doll."

Bill tried to defend Louise, but the more he said, the more sarcastic Lettie became.

"What I want to know is where you two went before you dived into the water?"

Louise ignored the question. "I'll say good night now, Bill. I enjoyed talking with you." She hurried through a rear door of the inn and up the back stairway to her room.

As she removed her wet clothes, Louise thought, "This just isn't my evening. The best thing for me to do is get into bed and read."

Meanwhile, Jean and Chris had left the dance and were standing on the porch of the inn, talking. In a few moments Doris joined them.

"Where's Bing?" Jean asked Doris.

"Oh, he received a telephone call. Then he came and told me he had to leave for a little while. He said he'd see me later in the evening and was terribly sorry he had to go."

Jean could not help but wonder where Bing had gone. Did it have something to do with the mystery of Horizon? But Bing seemed so nice—not a bit underhanded. Even his severe warning to her, Louise, and their dates to stay away from the lighthouse was probably given in the spirit of friendship. Jean put all suspicious thoughts out of her mind.

"No telling when he'll get back," said Doris, "so I think I'll go to bed."

"Oh, don't do that," Jean said. "Why don't the three of us walk down the beach?"

Doris agreed and the three set off. The girls took off their shoes and walked in bare feet. Unconsciously the young people found themselves headed toward the lighthouse. They decided to keep going until they reached the old building which stood in utter darkness.

"The girls, Ken, and I learned this comes under the restoration project," Chris told Doris.

"I wonder when they will start fixing it up," Doris mused.

Suddenly Jean exclaimed, "A ship! I wonder if it's the mysterious yacht we saw before!"

Doris asked what she meant and Jean told her the story. As they watched, it was quite evident that the vessel was not moving. A few minutes later a light on the foredeck began to flash signals.

"It's not Morse code," Chris announced. "Must be some private code."

"I wonder what the message is," Jean said, "and who she's signaling."

The disk of light continued to flash on and off, but it was fully five minutes before there was an answer. The response came from the tower of the lighthouse!

The three onlookers watched intently. "The guy in the lighthouse," Chris remarked, "isn't using Morse code either. In fact, I'd say all he's doing is swinging the light round and round."

There was an answering signal from the small ship, then the signaling stopped.

"Let's edge closer to the lighthouse and see who comes out of it," Jean urged.

The three ran through the sand as quickly as they could and waited for the person in the tower to emerge. No one appeared.

"Maybe he saw or heard us," Doris suggested, "and won't come out until we've gone."

"You could be right," Chris agreed. "What say we hide behind one of the sand dunes and continue to watch?"

The three pretended to retrace their steps, but once out of sight of the lighthouse they rounded a dune and took up watch. They remained for fifteen minutes but nothing happened.

"Either that signaler escaped through the trap door, or he's still in the building," Jean said. She felt that without a flashlight they would be at a disadvantage even if they did go inside to investigate.

The trio was disappointed. Jean heaved a sigh, then said, "We may as well go back to the inn."

By this time the mysterious ship was out of sight. Where had it come from and would it return again?

The first person they met upon reaching the inn was Bing Master. He looked at Doris a bit reproachfully.

"I've been searching all over for you," he said. "How about a dance?"

"Oh, I'm sorry, Bing," she apologized. "Yes, I'd love to dance."

The couple excused themselves and went off to the crowded, music-filled room. Shortly Jean and Chris also began to dance. A little while later they went to the snack room.

"I could go for a tall ice-cream soda," Chris remarked. "How about you?"

Jean said she would settle for root beer with vanilla ice cream. Since there were so many people milling around, the two did not talk about the mystery nor what they had seen that evening. Later, when Jean reached her room, she told Louise the full story.

"How exciting!" her sister said. "If you hadn't told me Bing was waiting for Doris at the inn, I would have suspected him of being the signaler. He seemed a bit nervous when he found us at the lighthouse."

"You know," said Jean, "I've been suspicious of him, too, but he really is such a nice guy. And besides, we don't have a shred of evidence against Bing Master."

Louise agreed. Then she described her own adventure and Lettie's irritated disbelief.

Jean laughed merrily. "I'm sorry I missed the show," she said.

The next morning, before the Danas left their room, Louise called State Police Headquarters and inquired if Mack and Mike had been apprehended. They were disappointed to hear that the men had not been captured.

"But we're busy on the case," the captain assured Louise.

She told him the girls had talked to Mr. Uhler, who vouched for the men's honesty. To herself Louise said, "Maybe none of the citizens of Horizon would turn Mack and Mike in, even if the men were seen stealing." She recalled the thieves' confidence in some sort of protection. Maybe the residents, like the employees at the inn, had also been threatened and were living in nightmarish fear.

As soon as breakfast was over, she discussed her suspicions with Jean. Then the two went to Mr. Olney's office. They wanted to find out if he had learned anything about the source of recent threats made to the inn's waitresses and chambermaids.

"And I think we ought to ask him about the ship, the lighthouse, and the signaling. Maybe he can offer some explanation," Louise suggested.

When they entered his office, he arose politely and asked them to sit down. He did not smile, however, and seemed unhappy and worried.

"I had no cooperation from the constable," he reported.

To their question about the mysterious signaling, he said he knew nothing about it and had heard no rumors regarding the ship or the lighthouse.

"I'm relatively new in this region," he said. "Believe me, if I had known when I bought this place what I know now, I never would have come here."

"What do you mean?" Jean asked.

"It is almost impossible to run the inn," he said. "I try to buy some of my supplies in town, but I find they short-weight me and make substitutions in my order. Fortunately I can buy most everything in Lawrenceville, where the problem doesn't exist. But the people in this village seem so smug. Sometimes I wonder if maybe they're causing me trouble deliberately."

Mr. Olney went on to say that within the past hour he had had a new bit of bad luck. "My porters received warnings similar to those given to the waitresses and chambermaids. Now they have walked out."

Louise and Jean glanced at each other in dismay. Apparently somebody was trying to ruin Mr. Olney's business. But why? The inn, so pleasantly situated, could draw hundreds of vacationers, making Horizon thrive again.

"Do you have one of the porter's letters?" Louise asked.

Mr. Olney opened a desk drawer and handed an envelope to her. To his surprise the young sleuth smelled the envelope. Then she pulled out the inside sheet and smelled that also.

"Why are you doing that?" the inn owner asked.

CHAPTER XII

Strange Villagers

LOUISE handed the envelope and note to Mr. Olney. "How does it smell to you?"

The inn owner sniffed the paper. "I can't smell anything but salt."

"Exactly," Louise told him. "Notice also that the paper is crinkled."

"Yes," Mr. Olney agreed. "Does that mean something?"

Both girls nodded. By now Jean knew what her sister suspected, but the inn owner still looked puzzled.

"I don't know a thing about detective work," he said. "Please tell me what conclusion you draw from this salty-smelling paper."

Louise told him that the letter had not been brought from inland. Rather, it had been exposed to sea air for some time.

"You mean this note was typed somewhere nearby."

"I believe so."

This announcement caused the inn owner to frown anxiously. It was bad enough, he said, to have apparent enemies in the village, but to have them right in his own establishment was disastrous.

Jean suggested that Mr. Olney investigate the credentials of every guest and employee. "Whoever is distributing these warnings may be the tool of someone else with other motives in mind. I'm convinced there is more than one man behind the trouble."

"I suppose you're right," the inn owner said. He heaved a great sigh. "I bought this place hoping to make an attractive spot that would become very popular. All my plans seem to be going wrong."

The Danas did what they could to persuade him not to be discouraged. They told him how wonderful the house-party guests thought the inn was.

Louise added, "As soon as the trouble is cleared up, hundreds of people will come flocking here."

Finally Mr. Olney smiled. "I hope you're right. And please keep on trying to solve the mystery."

The two girls promised to do their best and left. When they were in their room again, Jean said, "Louise, I have a hunch those warning letters were typed on that mystery ship."

"If you're right," her sister answered, "perhaps

we should notify the Coast Guard to find out about that yacht and its owner. I was going to suggest we do this when you told me of the odd signaling. But, on second thought, decided against it. If the coastal authorities found nothing wrong, we'd feel pretty foolish."

"And we really don't have much to tell them," Jean said. "Lots of ships go up and down this coast. I have an idea. Why don't we try to borrow or rent binoculars?"

"You mean we ought to try getting more information about the ship before we report it?" Louise asked.

"Yes."

The young detectives wondered if anyone at Horizon Inn had binoculars to lend them. They phoned Mr. Olney to find out.

"Sorry I can't help you," he said. "No one in the office has binoculars."

The Danas had not noticed any of the guests using binoculars. It seemed likely that some of the townspeople of Horizon would have field glasses. At least one of the residents would surely be interested in watching the ships passing on the ocean. They decided to make some inquiries in town.

Louise phoned Ken and Chris and told them the plan. The boys agreed it was a good idea and said they would meet the girls in the lobby for the trek to town.

When they reached the village, the two couples

took opposite sides of the street to make their inquiry. They knocked on door after door and stopped passers-by. Unfortunately none owned binoculars. One man remarked that the only shop that might carry that "sort o' paraphernalia" was several miles away.

Discouraged, the four young people headed for the constable's home. The front door was opened by Mr. Ritter himself. He was wearing a bathrobe and his callers assumed he probably had just got out of bed.

"Good morning," said Louise, and the others echoed the greeting.

"Mornin'," he responded. "For city folks you sure get up early. What do you want?"

Louise smiled. "Please don't think me presumptuous," she said, "but we didn't bring binoculars with us, and wondered if by any chance you had a pair we could borrow or rent."

The constable eyed the group suspiciously. "What is it you want to look at?"

"Oh, the ocean liners that go up and down," Louise replied casually.

Mr. Ritter rolled his eyes and puckered his lips as he thought this over.

Finally he said, "I ain't got any glasses and nobody else in this town does, either. Now see here. It seems to me that you folks are gettin' mighty inquisitive. Why don't you stay at the inn, have a good time, and stop your snoopin'?"

Jean flared up, "What makes you think we're snooping?"

"Oh, I hear things," the constable replied. "Go home and mind your own business!" He slammed the door.

For a moment the young people were angry, then suddenly they all burst into laughter. Formerly they had only suspected that the sleepy constable might be mixed up in the mystery of the troubled restoration of Horizon. Now they were sure of it.

As they turned to leave, the Danas and their friends noticed an elderly sailor standing in the road as if waiting to speak to them.

"Old Ritter tellin' you off?" he asked as they approached. A broad grin was spread over his face.

"Well, I guess you might call it that," Ken answered.

"Don't pay any attention to him," the sailor told them. "Ritter's grumpy most o' the time. It's a good thing we don't have no crime in this town. He sure couldn't get there quick enough to handle it."

"But there is crime in this town," Jean countered. "What about all of the thievery and sabotage?"

The sailor shrugged. "It's no business o' mine. I heard you askin' Ritter if he had binoculars. I got a powerful spyglass down in my cottage. I'd be glad to lend it to you."

"Oh, that would be cool!" said Jean. "Could we get it now?"

"Sure thing. Come along. My name's Pete Peterson. Just call me Pete."

When Louise introduced herself and the others, Sailor Pete commented, "You're a mighty fine-lookin' bunch. You stayin' at the inn?" They nodded.

Pete Peterson led them to his small weather-beaten cottage not far from the sand dunes. He explained that since retiring he enjoyed living alone and watching the ships.

"I used to work on a sailin' vessel when I was a boy," he told his visitors. "And I'm tellin' you, these fancy ocean liners can't come up to a full-rigged schooner. They ain't got the romance and adventure. I allus say a man's got to be a man to sign up on a sailin' ship."

Conversation finally turned to the phantom surfer and Louise asked Pete Peterson if he had heard or believed the story and if he had ever seen the ghost.

"I ain't never seen the phantom surfer, 'cause I like to go to bed early," the old sailor replied. "But I don't doubt the story. Why, many a time while I was on sailin' vessels and steamers I seen plenty o' ghosts."

"On your ship?" Chris asked.

"Yes. On my ship and sometimes I seen 'em walkin' right on the water."

The young people wanted to laugh, but their host was so serious they restrained themselves.

Suddenly he asked, "Have you seen the phantom surfer?"

"Yes, we have," Ken replied, but did not go into detail.

Pete Peterson began to chuckle. "So you want my spyglass to get a better look at him, eh?"

"It would certainly help us find out if he's real or an illusion," Jean answered.

She said nothing about the mysterious ship. If the old sailor always went to bed early, he would not have seen the flashing signals.

Pete took the spyglass from the case, trained it out a window, and then handed it to his visitors. In an instant they got a close-up view of a fishing vessel which had been a mere speck before.

"This is cool!" Jean remarked. "We appreciate your lending the spyglass to us. We'll take very good care of it."

The old sailor put it back in the case, fastened the clasp, and handed it to her.

When the young couples reached the inn, Jean said she would hide the spyglass in her room and bring it with her that evening. The girls proposed that they put on swimsuits after lunch and stroll back to the lighthouse.

"This time we'll take along a couple of flashlights," Louise said.

The Danas hurried off to help with the preparations for lunch. Mr. Olney had still not been able to engage new waitresses. Lettie Briggs and her group had not appeared for any meals since the walkout.

"I wish she'd move out of here," Jean said in disgust.

At two-thirty the Danas met Ken and Chris. They decided it would be wise to take a more discreet route to the lighthouse, one that was out of sight of the beach. They left the inn by the rear door and started toward town. The Briggs' car whizzed past them, evidently just returning from luncheon in the country.

"Well, Bill is still here," Louise said.

Ken laughed. "Maybe it's because of the good food."

At a bend in the road, the two couples turned left across the weed-grown sandy dunes. As the lighthouse came in sight, Chris started down a steep embankment. Suddenly he lost his balance, sat down, and slid.

Near the foot of the dune there was a large clump of bushes. Ken thought they would stop his fall, but instead the whole mass of beach shrubs were pulled down with him. He landed on the sand, got to his feet, and then stared in amazement. Before him was a padlocked wooden door which had been screened by the brush.

His companions leaped down to join him.

"Look!" he exclaimed. "A secret door! It must lead to something inside the dune!"

"Private—Keep Out" had been painted on the door in large letters.

"It doesn't say who the owner is," Ken remarked. "If the town is, I'm sure there'd be an official sign on it to that effect."

Meanwhile Jean had been surveying the door with interest. Finally she burst out, "I'll bet this is the place we've been searching for all along!"

"What do you mean?" Chris asked.

Jean said excitedly, "It may be a hideout for the phantom surfer!"

CHAPTER XIII

Flying Feet

THE young people stared at the door in the dune and wondered what lay behind it. Was it just a storage compartment belonging to a fisherman? Ken and Chris were inclined to agree with their dates that something mysterious was concealed. Otherwise, why would anyone bother to camouflage the door with brush?

"We had better pile the bushes back where they were," Louise said.

"Right," Jean agreed. "And I also think we should cover our footprints that lead to the entrance."

"And fill in the trough you made, Chris, when you slid down the slope," Ken added.

Before setting the brush in place, the boys used it like brooms to sweep away all traces of their approach. Then they adjusted the great pile in front of the door, hiding it completely.

Chris began to laugh. "I feel as much like a criminal as I do a sleuth," he declared. "Which role are you girls trying to teach us?"

"Well," Jean replied, "which do you prefer—jail or fun?"

Her date grinned. "I'll just settle for adventure."

The two couples walked across the shell-strewn beach and climbed onto the promontory that led out to the lighthouse.

"After so many visits to this place," said Ken, "I'm beginning to feel quite at home. Of course I'd have to get permission from the Osbornes, but maybe next time I'll just bring a sleeping bag and camp out."

"That might not be such a bad idea," Louise told him. "It would save you a lot of walking."

"Would you bring all my meals to me?" he teased.

Louise's eyes sparkled. "Would you settle for one a day?"

There was more joking and teasing, but as they came to the entrance of the lighthouse everyone sobered. They went inside, closed the door gently, and looked around. Nothing had been disturbed. The rope lay coiled in the same place and the trap door was shut.

Ken and Chris would not allow the girls to accompany them into the watery tunnel. They took off their beach robes and slippers, then opened the trap door.

"I don't think we'll need to use the rope this time," Chris put in as he peered into the calm depths below.

"You girls stand guard," Ken told them, then followed his friend down the slippery rungs.

Each boy carried a waterproof flashlight strapped to his arm. Every necessary precaution was taken. Within half a minute the beams vanished and the girls could see only the yawning hole below them.

As they waited, the Danas suddenly became alert. They had heard a noise at the main door. The next moment it began to open slowly. Their hearts pounded faster. Who was coming? Friend or enemy?

What should they do? Instinctively they tiptoed down the ladder and Louise noiselessly set the trap door in place. But she raised one side of it an inch so she could peek out.

A moment later the entrance door was swung open. In bounded a large black dog. He began to bark furiously but kept wagging his tail, so the Danas knew he was harmless. Apparently he had scented their presence. No one followed him inside.

The girls burst into laughter and came out of their hiding place. Jean held one hand toward the dog in a friendly gesture.

"Hello, old fella!" she said. "Come over and see us."

The collarless animal needed no second invitation. Wagging his tail so hard that his hindquarters swayed from side to side, the friendly brown-eyed dog moved closer to be patted.

"Are you alone?" Louise asked. "Or is somebody waiting outside for you?"

She had never seen this dog and wondered to whom he belonged. Louise stepped to the entrance and looked up and down the expansive beach and across the sand dunes. She saw no one.

"I guess he came by himself," Louise reported to her sister. "But we'd better not leave the entrance to the tunnel open." They closed it.

After another ten minutes had gone by, the girls felt sure that nobody was coming for the dog, so they lifted the iron cover. They were just in time because the two boys were now ascending the ladder.

"Did you find anything?" Louise asked them.

"No," Chris answered, "we didn't find the king's ransom."

"Or anything else," Ken added, "but we did get all the way to the end of the tunnel. It's continually covered by the spray of breaking waves. Only an expert swimmer or surfer could possibly survive in there."

"But," Chris said, "why a person would want to take his life in his hands in such a fashion is beyond me. I'll swim and surf in safer waters, thank you."

His remark started Louise thinking. Anyone attempting such a dangerous maneuver must be after a very valuable prize. It was frustrating not to be able to fit together the links of the puzzle.

"But I'll do it!" she determined.

Suddenly Louise wondered why the boys had not mentioned the dog and why the animal had not barked. She whirled around, calling to him, but their visitor had left.

"What's with you?" Ken said to Louise. "Has this mystery made you stir crazy?"

"No, sir." She smiled and added, "Jean and I just met another phantom."

The boys looked shocked. Grinning, Louise described the black hound's mystery visit.

Chris laughed. "Guess he didn't like us, Ken."

His friend grinned. "Let's go!" he suggested.

Jean asked the others to wait a minute. "I think we should investigate the tower. It just occurred to me that the dog might have been looking for his master. And that person could be upstairs."

Ken went up and reported that the place was empty. "All clear," he said. "And the scarf is still there."

To keep their trip to the lighthouse a secret, the four young people took the same route away from the beach that led to the back of the inn. In a short time they were on the beach with the rest of their friends. They discovered that Lettie Briggs had spread a story about the Danas' and their dates' trip to town "in their beach robes."

Louise and Jean were amused by Lettie's silly tale while Ken and Chris chose to ignore it and were glad to learn the Starhurst house party had done the same.

Apparently tired from their tunnel exploration, the boys sprawled out on a blanket to sun themselves.

Louise and Jean, however, wanted to cool off in the surf. After a refreshing swim, they shampooed and dried their hair in the beach house. By now they were ready to continue work on the mystery.

Jean said, "Why don't we go to Horizon again and look around a little?"

"Okay. We didn't have a chance this morning to find out if there has been any more damage or thievery," Louise replied.

"Let's tell the boys." She scooped up a handful of water and giggled. "In case they need some reviving, I'll use this." Her sister grinned and did the same.

Making sure none of it spilled, they ran back toward Ken and Chris.

"Hey, sunfish," Jean teased as she and Louise poured the cold water onto the boys' reddening backs. "How about some more exercise?"

"Oh, that's what you want?" Ken winked at Chris.

In a flash the two picked up the girls and ran toward the ocean. Frantically the sisters flailed their arms and legs, trying to avoid an untimely dunking.

"Stop, please!" Louise cried. "My hair—"

In reply he nodded to his cohort and continued wading into deeper water. "Let's see if we can catch that wave, Chris."

In a matter of seconds the boys had dropped the helpless girls onto a long, smooth curl, causing a tremendous splash.

"Oh, you make me so mad, Chris Barton!" Jean spluttered as she arose.

Louise also continued to scold, but her words were swallowed up by the sound of gushing spray. She and Jean began to take long, quick strokes toward the shore. The boys followed.

When the foursome reached the dry sand, Chris remarked, "Where's that old fun spirit, kids?"

Louise replied that she and Jean had just fixed their hair preparatory to revisiting Horizon. Immediately the boys declared their eagerness to accompany them into town.

As the four plodded to the inn they passed Lettie Briggs and her group. Bill smiled but Lettie merely smirked.

She said to him, "Those four make me ill. So juvenile in their actions, don't you think?"

Her friends did not reply but Bill winked at Louise.

After a quick change of clothes, the Danas and their dates walked up the road to the village. They noticed that very little restoration work had been done. Finally they came to a lovely old house which seemed to have been neglected for a long time.

"I can imagine how beautiful it must have been once," Louise murmured. "Wouldn't it be exciting to—"

Her sentence went unfinished and the stillness around them was suddenly shattered by a booming voice.

"*Clear the area at once! Hurry!*"

The two couples looked at each other. Was this a hoax?

Before they had a chance to move, they heard a terrific explosion inside the old house. It shook as if a hurricane wind had hit it. The next moment its doors and windows blew out and debris flew everywhere.

The impact lifted the boys and girls off the ground and hurled them some distance away! Then, within seconds, the whole catastrophe was over.

Stunned and shaken, the Danas and their friends picked themselves up. By this time residents were running up the street to see what had happened and if anyone were hurt. The young people told them about the explosion and assured them they were all right.

"Have you any idea what caused it?" one woman asked.

"Somebody must have planted a bomb in the house," cried an irate man and continued to sputter angrily, "What's this town coming to?"

The impact hurled them some distance away!

Ambling slowly up the street and seemingly unexcited were Constable Ritter and another man.

"Now maybe we'll get some action," said another citizen. "Here comes Mayor Canby and the constable."

When they arrived at the scene, John Ritter hardly looked at the ruined building. Instead, his eyes fastened on the four young people.

"Mayor," he said, "here are those snoopers I was tellin' you about. I wouldn't put it past 'em to have caused the explosion. In fact," he said, glaring at them, "I have half a mind to run 'em in."

"On what charge?" Ken asked angrily.

The mayor answered. "You've been told to stay away from this project. Maybe the only way to keep you from meddling is to lock you up." The bushy-browed, hard-eyed man glared at them.

Louise and Jean were disgusted at the attitude of the two officials. They showed no concern about the explosion nor the house which was included in the restoration program. The Danas guessed that Mayor Canby and Constable Ritter knew who the perpetrator was and were shielding him.

Louise and Jean had been listening intently to the voices of everyone surrounding them and made a point of speaking to all the men. Not one voice could be identified as belonging to the person who had boomed out the warning. Had the man disguised his voice? the girls wondered. They noted that Mr. Uhler was not among the onlookers.

Meanwhile, Ken and Chris had also walked away from the mayor and the constable. They wondered if the scattered debris might contain some clue to the cause of the explosion.

They were about ready to give up their search when Ken suddenly cried out, "Over there! That looks like another bomb!"

CHAPTER XIV

Spyglass View

AT Ken's warning the whole crowd fled in various directions.

Some of them began to shout at other people who were arriving. "Get out! Run! There's a live bomb here!"

When everyone was at a safe distance, Louise and Jean looked around for the mayor and the constable. They were standing together a little distance from everyone else. Both of them were laughing as if they were enjoying some joke.

"How can they be so hilarious with such a dangerous situation at their doorstep?" Louise fumed.

"I'm going to speak to them!" Jean said, and started toward the officials.

Louise hurried off with her. When they reached the men, Jean said, "Have you any idea, Mr. Canby, who is responsible for leaving the bomb?"

The men looked at the two girls in annoyance,

but Canby replied, "If I did, I wouldn't share the information with a couple of schoolgirls. I've heard you're amateur detectives, but I want to tell you I don't need your help. I strongly advise you to stay at the inn for the rest of your vacation."

The constable added, "Don't come into town again and don't wander away from Mr. Olney's property."

The Danas were embarrassed and annoyed. Before walking off, Louise asked, "Aren't you going to deactivate the bomb?"

By this time the constable's face was red with anger, but he kept his voice steady. "If it hasn't gone off by now, it ain't likely to."

"That's right," Mayor Canby put in. "And don't you worry, girls. We'll keep our eyes open for anybody suspicious."

The Danas joined their dates. As they walked back to the inn, Jean remarked, "Well, we almost went to jail!"

"That constable's a big blowhard," Ken remarked. "He wouldn't dare. We'd fight and the proceedings might show him up."

The two couples discussed the latest bit of sabotage to the restoration. Chris remarked, "Whoever is trying to ruin the project is making a good job of it."

"But what *is* the reason?" Ken asked. "It looks as if the town's leaders are involved."

Louise said that one thing puzzled her. Had the

deep-voiced man who had given the warning seen their group coming and called out? Or would he have given the warning in any case?

Ken replied, "That may be something we'll never find out. I'm thankful he gave it at all. At least we were alerted, even though we didn't have a chance to run."

Conversation turned to the unexploded bomb. "Surely the mayor and the constable wouldn't leave it to explode," Louise remarked. "Their own lives would be in danger!"

"Don't worry," Ken replied. "Mayor Canby strikes me as the kind of man who won't take suggestions from anybody, but wouldn't be foolish enough to risk his own neck. He'll get somebody to deactivate the bomb for him."

After the four had reached the inn, they changed into swimsuits and went out on the beach. A great crowd had gathered in one spot.

"I wonder what happened," said Jean, starting to run.

The others followed her. As they reached the spot, a young man called out, "Stand back! Give her air!"

Someone must have had an accident!

"Who is it?" Jean asked a girl standing nearby.

"I don't know her name. She's with the Starhurst group. She almost drowned!"

The Danas' hearts began to pound. Was it Doris? Or Evelyn? They must find out!

The victim proved to be Lettie Briggs. Pale and bedraggled, she was sitting up now and leaning against Bill Potter. Instead of looking frightened or worried, Lettie seemed very happy.

She gazed up at Louise with a flippant toss of her head as if to say, "You thought you got my boy friend away from me. You see how mistaken you are."

"I'm sorry you had such a scare," Louise told her.

Lettie did not reply. Instead she snuggled against Bill, who appeared to be embarrassed.

"If you feel all right now, Lettie," he said, "I think you'd better go up to the inn. I'll help you."

He assisted the girl to her feet and looked relieved when her mother met them on the porch. News of the near-fatal accident had reached her and she insisted that Lettie come with her and go to bed at once. Bill, free of his responsibility, hurried back to the beach.

In the meantime, Doris was telling the Danas and their dates what had happened. Lettie had finally inveigled Bing into giving her a lesson on the surfboard.

"She disobeyed every instruction he gave her. The result was she wiped out in deep water and then panicked because she felt herself being carried seaward."

Lettie, unable to battle the wave, had gone

under. Bing had rescued her, and with Bill Potter helping, had given Lettie first aid. Fortunately she had responded quickly.

Bing walked over to the Danas' group. He heard the end of Doris's recital.

When she stopped speaking, he said, "I wouldn't give Lettie Briggs another lesson if she paid me a hundred dollars for it."

Chris grinned. "Bet she won't even go in the water!"

Louise and Jean took a quick dip and one ride each on a surfboard, then went to their room. Evelyn came in and asked what the girls had seen in Horizon. When she heard about the explosion, her eyes popped.

"Why, you might have been killed!" Evelyn exclaimed. "Please don't go up there any more."

"Maybe we won't have to," Louise said soothingly. "At least not until we return this spyglass."

Jean added, "I'm beginning to think we're not going to solve the mystery in town."

"Then where?" Evelyn asked.

"Probably around the lighthouse."

She showed Evelyn the telescope and told her about the kindly old sailor who had lent it to the sisters.

"He sounds interesting," Evelyn remarked. "So he declares he has seen ghosts walking on the ocean!" She chuckled. "Then with his spyglass, girls, you certainly ought to be able to see the phantom surfer!"

She walked to the window and put the telescope to one eye. The next moment she burst out laughing.

"What do you see?" Louise asked.

Evelyn continued to giggle and did not answer right away. But finally she handed the telescope to Jean. When she looked into it, she too burst into laughter.

"Let me see," said Louise. "What's the joke? Something on the beach?"

As the other two stood by with broad grins on their faces, Louise adjusted the spyglass.

"Oh no!" she exclaimed, and then joined the others in uncontrolled giggles.

"I can't say the bear looks like you," said Evelyn. "But where did he get those clothes?"

The girls had discovered that someone had taped a transparency to the end of the spyglass. It was a picture of a dressed-up dancing bear. Underneath had been scrawled *Louise*.

"I suppose this is some more of Lettie's work," Jean said. "She must have sneaked in here and pasted this on."

"Well, at least this time it wasn't mean," Louise remarked. "And I must say it's funny." She laughed again.

Louise took one more look, then untaped the

transparency. She wiped off the magnifying glass with a damp cloth, and then looked through the instrument again.

"An ocean liner is just going by," she told the others.

The girls took turns looking at various ships steaming up and down the coast. None of them was the yacht which had anchored in the vicinity of the lighthouse.

"I guess the mystery ship stops here only at night," Louise concluded.

She and Jean changed their clothes quickly and went down to the dining room to help with preparations for the evening meal. As soon as their chores were finished, they went back to dress for the evening dance.

"Wow! Here comes a movie star!" Ken commented as Louise appeared in a stunning pale-green dress.

Jean received a similar compliment from Chris who added, "I like that groovy hairdo."

After dinner the Danas and their dates spent about an hour on the dance floor.

When it became dark, Jean whispered to the others, "Let's leave now and change our clothes so we'll be ready for our visit to the lighthouse. This time we'll take the spyglass along and get some close-ups."

The boys agreed and the four left one by one so it would not seem too obvious to others that they planned to disappear together. Louise stopped to chat with Doris, and Jean went off to tell Evelyn their plans. "Pass the word along to the Osbornes, will you?"

"Glad to. And do be careful."

Louise and Jean met at the door leading from the outdoor dance floor to the lobby. On their way to the stairs, the girls' attention was suddenly arrested by a large sign. It was thumbtacked to the wooden wall.

The Danas looked at each other in dismay. The sign read:

POSITIVELY NO STROLLING
ON THE BEACH AFTER DARK

CHAPTER XV

Sneaking Figures

"Nobody can go on the beach at night!" Jean exclaimed. "What's the big idea?"

Louise was staring at the sign on the lobby wall. She pointed out to her sister that the order was unsigned.

"That's funny," Jean remarked. "Do you suppose Mr. Olney tacked it up?"

At that moment they saw the owner of the inn on the porch and went to ask him. "Sign?" he asked. "I didn't put any up."

He followed the girls into the lobby and stared at it, perplexed. Then he walked over to Mr. Voss, the night desk clerk, and asked if he had seen anyone thumbtacking the notice to the wall.

The young man shook his head. "Not while I was here. I was away from the desk for about five minutes half an hour ago. Maybe the person hung the sign then."

Jean spoke up. "Were there any guests around when you left the desk?"

Mr. Voss shook his head. "Everybody was at dinner."

The Danas concluded that someone had sneaked in while the lobby was empty. But who was it?

Ken and Chris had come into the lobby and had remained silent, but now Ken said, "Someone obviously wants to keep us away from the vicinity of the activities of himself and his friends."

"And that's the beach," Chris added.

Mr. Olney looked worried. "Maybe you should obey the sign then and avoid danger."

"Perhaps," Louise said.

The four young people left the owner and the desk clerk talking about what to do with the sign. Should they take it down or leave it up—at least for this evening?

The Danas and their friends walked out to the porch and gazed up and down the beach. All of them felt sure that whoever wanted to keep hotel guests off the beach was connected with the mystery.

Chris remarked, "This convinces me that the crooks will be operating at night."

"I agree," said Jean. "And that means if we're going to solve the mystery, as Mr. Olney has asked us to do, we'll have to work on it after dark."

Ken said he recommended that they pay no attention to the sign. He grinned. "Our objective is the lighthouse. We don't have to go down the beach to reach it."

Louise smiled. "That's right. We can take the back route across the sand dunes."

She told the others that she had asked Evelyn to inform the Osbornes of their plan.

At once Jean said, "If they should see that sign in the lobby, maybe they'll forbid our going."

"We'll have to take that chance," Louise told her. "After all there is an element of danger in what we're doing and somebody at the inn, especially our chaperones, should know where we are in case of trouble. I think I'd better tell them about the sign and ask their permission."

The others nodded and Louise went off to find the Osbornes. They were playing cards.

In a whisper Louise told Mrs. Osborne what the four young people would like to do, despite the mysterious warning. After briefly discussing the matter with her husband and exacting a promise that the girls would be extremely careful, she gave her consent.

"Please don't go anywhere except to the lighthouse," Mrs. Osborne requested.

By ten-thirty Louise and Jean and their dates had changed into hiking clothes and met at the rear entrance of the inn. Louise was carrying the spyglass and all had flashlights. Dancing was still in progress and the Danas were delighted to see Bing and Doris enjoying it.

"They have certainly hit it off," Louise remarked.

Jean chuckled. "Charlie had better watch his step!"

At once Ken said with a grin, "I'll warn him as soon as we get back."

The four sleuths set off in a gay mood, but as they started across the sand dunes toward the lighthouse, conversation turned to more serious matters.

"I wonder if the phantom surfer will be out tonight," Jean said.

Chris asked, "Didn't we last see him on a clear night? The sky is very overcast now and he'd have a hard time cutting his way through the water."

Jean giggled. "Would this make any difference to a phantom?"

"I guess not," Chris conceded, grinning.

Reaching a good vantage point from which to watch the ocean, the promontory, the lighthouse and the beach, the four sleuths stopped and conversation ceased for some time. The only noise was made by the crashing waves. No one was in sight. The phantom surfer did not appear and not a ship went past.

"Looks as if we've drawn a blank," Ken said in a whisper.

The others did not answer because at that very moment they had detected a tiny light near the end of the promontory.

"Someone's coming out of the lighthouse!" Louise announced excitedly.

The watchers strained their eyes to distinguish the figure and see what was going on. One man, followed by another, emerged from the building. Each was carrying a flashlight. It was impossible to determine what they looked like.

Louise took the spyglass from its case and trained it on the men. In the darkness she could not see their faces.

"I wonder what the men were doing in there," Ken said.

"Your guess is as good as mine," Louise answered. "One thing is certain. They haven't signaled from the tower since we've been here." She looked at her watch and added, "In the past twenty minutes."

The watchers took turns looking through the spyglass as the shadowy figures made their way along the promontory to the beach. When the two reached it, they stopped to confer.

"Maybe they're planning to stop at that secret entrance in the sand dune," Jean suggested.

A few moments later the men came in that direction. The Danas and their friends hurried forward and hid on a dune next to the one where the door was.

"If the men stop there, what'll we do?" Jean whispered.

"Move in," Chris replied.

To their disappointment the pair went right past the door, climbed onto the dune, and walked off across the grassy hillocks of sand. Unfortunately they had the collars of their bulky slickers turned up and their hats pulled low so that their faces could not be seen.

Chris heaved a sigh. "Nothing suspicious about those men."

Jean laughed softly. "What proof have you, Detective Barton?"

"Just the same," Louise spoke up, "I'd like to follow them."

As the four were about to set off, Ken exclaimed, "Look! There's that mysterious ship!"

Its lights had suddenly appeared. Had the yacht been there all the time? Or had it been running in darkness and just arrived?

Louise trained the spyglass on the ship and could vaguely glimpse figures moving on the deck. A mist lay over the water and it was impossible to make out anything clearly. She was not able to distinguish a name on the side of the vessel nor letters nor insignia on the one smokestack.

"I can't see any identifying mark," Louise reported. "Ken, you try."

He had no better luck. Jean and Chris took turns but confessed it was hopeless to pierce the atmosphere.

"That's too bad," Ken remarked, shaking his head. "Otherwise we could have reported it to the Coast Guard."

Suddenly all the lights on the yacht went out. Though the young people anxiously waited another fifteen minutes, the lights did not reappear.

"It's my guess," said Louise, "that the yacht steamed off, running without lights until it's safely out of sight of anyone who might possibly be watching from here. No telling which direction it took."

Jean remarked that it had been a pretty fruitless evening. "We might have fared better if we had followed those two men."

"We could still try," Chris told her. "There hasn't been much of a breeze tonight so their footprints in the sand may not have been swept away yet. Maybe we could find them."

Beaming their flashlights, the trekkers started off. It was fairly easy to follow the men's marks, but Louise felt sure that when the two mysterious figures reached the road, footprints would be lost. Nevertheless, the couples pushed on, plodding with difficulty through the heavy sand.

Louise was in the lead. Suddenly she exclaimed, "I've found something! Maybe it's a clue!"

The others hurried to her side as she picked up a tightly bound package. There was no name or mark of any kind on it.

"Do you suppose those men dropped this?" Chris asked.

"Well, it's right here near their footprints," Louise replied.

"Let's open the package," Ken suggested.

Louise handed it to him. The others watched eagerly as he yanked hard at the stout string which was tied around it. Finally the cord came off and he began pulling back the several layers of paper.

"There must be something either fragile or valuable, or perhaps both, in here," he guessed.

Finally he uncovered the contents. Everyone stared in amazement, then in chorus they exclaimed:

"Money!"

CHAPTER XVI

Police Surprise

MANY questions raced through the minds of the Danas and their friends as they stared at the package of money. Had it been lost or dropped on purpose? Were the men they were trailing its owners?

"Maybe it was stolen!" Chris suggested.

"Could be," Ken agreed, then turned to Louise and Jean. "What do you think?"

"I can only guess," Louise replied. "Of course the first thing that comes to my mind is that it's just another piece in the puzzle of Horizon. But how it fits, I have no idea right now."

Jean suggested that perhaps stolen money was temporarily stashed at the lighthouse. "When the thieves think they're safe from a possible police hunt, they'll go there and take it all out."

Ken remarked, "If that is true and those two

dropped the pack of money, what a surprise they're in for when they discover it's missing!"

"Maybe they'll come back looking for the package," Chris spoke up. "Perhaps we should leave it here, hide, and wait for them."

Louise vetoed the idea. "I think if they were going to return they would have been here by now."

She and the others looked into the distance but could see no flashlights in evidence.

"Let's take this money to the inn and have Mr. Olney put it in the safe overnight," Louise suggested.

"And then what?" Ken asked.

"It should be turned over to the police. I wonder how much is here."

Ken counted the bills, then gasped in amazement.

"Wow! There's five thousand dollars!" he exclaimed.

"It's all new money, too," Chris pointed out.

The package was wrapped and tied again. Ken carried it. Several times the others jokingly asked him if he still had it.

Once he replied with a grin, "Why no. I hid it back in a sand dune."

Louise chuckled. "And how do you plan to spend it?"

Ken replied, "Tomorrow I'll return for the package and take off on a spending spree. I'll be the grooviest guy in Walton Academy!" The others laughed.

When the two girls and their dates reached the inn, Chris said, "Ken and I promised to help Bing on the surfboards tomorrow morning. Some of them need repairing. Others must have their skegs—that's fins—fixed, and most of them must be waxed."

Louise smiled. "We'll excuse you. Jean and I will take the money to State Police Headquarters at Hunter's Point. I suppose it should go to the constable but I don't trust him!"

"You really should have a bodyguard," Chris objected.

"Oh, we'll be all right," Jean insisted.

After the foursome described their recent adventure to the inn owner and the money had been put in the safe, the Danas went to their room. Almost immediately there was a knock on their door.

"Where in the world have you two been?" Doris queried as she and Evelyn walked in. "Bing has been worried about your absence."

"We're perfectly all right," Louise assured the girls.

She and Jean told them about their thrilling evening and said they thought the whole matter should be kept confidential.

"We won't say a word," Evelyn promised. "But what an experience! You're sure you'll be all right tomorrow? That's an awful lot of money for you to carry. How are you going to get to the State Police?"

The Danas said that they would rent a car. Early the next morning Louise telephoned a rental service in Lawrenceville and arranged for an attendant to bring a convertible to meet them just beyond the town of Horizon.

When he arrived at the designated spot, he said he would drive them all to the rental agency to fill out the necessary application. The girls found him to be very curious. On the ride to Lawrenceville, he asked who they were, why they were staying at the inn, where they went to school, and if they had boy friends. Finally, to their disgust, he offered to get another young man so they could double date together!

"Thank you but all our time is taken up," Louise replied in an icy tone.

Jean changed the subject abruptly. "Have you heard of the phantom surfer?"

"Sure."

"Ever seen him?" Jean went on.

"Nope. But a couple o' fellows I know have. Lots of people don't believe the story but I think it's true."

"Tell me," said Louise, "do most people here agree that it is a ghost?"

The young man nodded. "What else could it be?"

As the girls shrugged, he went on, "Do you

know I've been told that the phantom surfer comes right down out of the sky, rides the waves, and then disappears?"

Louise and Jean grinned. "That's quite a story," Jean commented.

By this time they had reached the automobile agency and Louise got out with the driver. After filling out the rental form, she took the wheel and headed for Hunter's Point. When they reached the thriving inland town, Louise asked a traffic policeman for directions to State Police Headquarters.

"It's about a mile from here," he said. "Just follow this road."

The girls thanked him and within minutes turned into the grounds where a sign pointed to the visitors' entrance. When they entered the main office, the Danas were directed to Captain Markham. He was very much interested in their story and opened the package at once.

He scrutinized the top bill intensely, then picked it up. Next he crumbled the bill between his fingers and finally pressed a buzzer on his desk.

A few seconds later another trooper walked in and was introduced as Sergeant Wilk. The captain asked him, "What do you think of this bill?"

The other officer took it and said almost at once, "It's counterfeit."

The Danas were stunned. Jean asked, "Is the whole package counterfeit?"

Sergeant Wilk examined the bills, then nodded. "Every one of them. I must say these are very good counterfeits. Whoever is making them is very skilled and alert to the finest details."

Captain Markham asked the girls to repeat their story to the sergeant.

"I'm sorry I can't give you any description of the men we think may have dropped the package," Louise said, "except that one was tall and the other short. Just like those lumber thieves, Mike and Mack, you're looking for."

"Even through our spyglass we couldn't distinguish their features," Jean spoke up.

The two officers looked surprised and the captain said, "You had a spyglass with you? Why?"

Louise told him they had been watching ships on the ocean. When they had spotted the pair coming toward the dunes, they had gazed at them through the glass.

Captain Markham did not ask any more questions. He rose and the girls said good-by to him.

"If you pick up anything else of importance, please bring it to us," he requested, smiling.

As the girls reached the center of town, Louise said, "I wonder if any of the shopkeepers here have received counterfeit bills."

"Let's ask in a few places," Jean proposed, and her sister pulled into a parking space.

The girls went into several stores and a small hotel. At each the answer to their query was No.

"How about the bank?" Louise suggested. She had seen the building when they rode into Hunter's Point.

The girls found it busy, with lines of customers at the tellers' windows. They went to the manager.

In response to Louise's question, the manager smiled and said, "No, we haven't seen any counterfeit bills around here, thank goodness. Anything else I can do for you?"

"No, thank you," Louise answered.

As she and Jean turned to leave the building, Jean grabbed her sister's arm. "Look who's over there!"

Two men had just entered the bank. Mayor Canby and Constable Ritter!

"What are they doing here?" Louise mused.

Jean grinned. "Maybe chasing us."

They could not get out of the bank without passing the men. Upon seeing the Danas, they stopped short and glared at them.

"Aren't you pretty far from home base?" the mayor asked them.

"Oh, it's not many miles from Horizon to Hunter's Point," Jean said nonchalantly.

"How did you get here?" the constable thundered at them. "I thought you didn't have a car."

Louise could not resist saying, "You keep pretty close tabs on us."

"Maybe I do," the constable replied. "It's my duty to know what's going on around Horizon."

The Danas could hardly keep from laughing. Did the sleepy old constable think he was on the job? They concluded that he was better at snooping than at detecting or apprehending.

Louise said, "We rented a car and drove over here."

"Why?" the mayor queried.

"To do a little shopping," Jean spoke up.

The two officials looked at each other as if to say, "We aren't going to learn a thing from these girls." The men evidently decided to give up, for without another word they stepped in line before one of the tellers' windows.

As the Danas walked up the street to their rented car, they continued to wonder why the men were in this particular town. There was a good bank in Lawrenceville. Why would they have come all the way to Hunter's Point to do their banking?

"I'm glad we got rid of those bills before we met them," said Louise, chuckling. "If Canby and Ritter had found out about the counterfeit money, they probably would have insisted we turn it over to them."

Jean nodded. "And I wouldn't put it past them to have kept it!"

Again Louise took the wheel of the car and this time headed directly for Horizon Inn. After they had ridden through Lawrenceville and were on the short cut, Jean suddenly said, "Slow down.

I see somebody in that lagoon over there. The swimmer seems to be in trouble."

Not far from them was a small body of water into which the ocean drained.

"Jean, that person needs help!" Louise exclaimed.

Instantly she turned off the highway, and headed the car across the bumpy terrain bordering the lagoon. A little girl was floundering in the water.

"Jean, she'll drown!"

The two girls jumped from the car, kicked off their shoes, and raced into the water. Swimming furiously, they reached the child just as she was going down again. They brought her to the surface and gently towed her to shore.

At once they laid the unconscious child face down and Louise applied artificial respiration. There was no response.

"Oh, Louise!" Jean cried. "We must save her!"

The two girls took turns trying to restore the child's breathing.

CHAPTER XVII

Eavesdropper!

FRANTIC, Louise and Jean worked steadily on the little girl.

When they did not get any response, Jean murmured, "Oh, Louise, this is awful!"

"We mustn't give up!" her sister answered.

Suddenly their efforts were rewarded. The little girl began to breathe again!

With sighs of relief they turned the child over onto her back. Presently she opened her eyes and stared vacantly at the girls. They did not talk to her, just smiled.

As color began to tinge her cheeks, she asked, "Who are you? How did I get here?"

"We brought you out of the water," Louise told her.

She took hold of the little girl's hand and patted it gently.

"You're going to be all right," Jean added. "We'll take you home. Where do you live?"

The little girl began to sob. She buried her face in her hands and her little body shook.

"Now don't feel bad," Louise coaxed. "You're a lucky little girl, but try to forget the whole thing."

"Oh, I can't forget!" the child wailed. "I—I was told not to come to this lagoon without a grown-up."

Jean pointed out that it was unfortunate she had been disobedient but not to worry any more.

"I'll be in trouble when I get home," the little girl said, and again burst into tears. "My name's Mary Murphy and I live in Horizon. My—my mommy will probably whip me."

The Danas did not comment on this. They hoped Mrs. Murphy would feel that the child had been so frightened she would not need any further punishment.

"Come, come, let's go!" Jean urged Mary.

The child stood up, her bathing suit now almost dry, and smiled at the Danas. "Thank you for saving me," she said.

Getting between them and linking arms, she added, "When we get home, please come into my house and talk to my mommy. Then maybe she won't scold me. You know, I can swim pretty good. I don't know what happened to me today."

The Danas wrung most of the water from their

skirts before they climbed into the car. Mary directed them to her home, a modest weather-beaten cottage. Again the child was insistent that the girls come inside.

"I think my daddy's home," she said. "He's a nice man. I have lots of fun with him, but nowadays he doesn't want to play with me much."

"I'm sorry," said Louise. "Is it perhaps because you are disobedient?"

"Oh no," Mary assured her. "Today is the first time I ever didn't mind."

As Mary opened the front door, a middle-aged man walked toward them. He looked astonished at his wet visitors.

"This is my daddy," Mary said, and told him how the girls had saved her from drowning.

"Oh Mary!" he said, hugging her. "How can I ever thank these young ladies?"

"Please don't," said Louise, adding, "We're Louise and Jean Dana on vacation at the inn."

"I hope you're having a good time," he said. "There isn't much to offer in Horizon by way of entertainment except ocean bathing."

The girls said they had found the place very interesting but mysterious. They asked him about the phantom surfer.

Mr. Murphy shrugged. "I don't know whether the story is true or not. Sometimes I think people who declare they've seen him are spoofing."

Mary's father said his wife was out and offered

to make a pot of tea for the girls. They thanked him but said No. Louise brought up the subject of the restoration.

At once Mr. Murphy's pleasant expression turned to one of despair. "I'm a carpenter—an honest one," he said. "You've probably heard that things aren't going well in town. I'm out of work more than I'm busy."

Mary's father went on to say that he was employed by Mr. Uhler, but time and time again work which he had done was destroyed overnight.

"Then I'm unemployed for a while."

"That's a shame," Jean spoke up. "Do you suspect anyone of sabotage?"

It was fully fifteen seconds before the carpenter replied. Then he said slowly, "You folks are strangers to me and perhaps I shouldn't speak my mind. But you look like honest girls who wouldn't go around repeating stories told to you in confidence."

"Indeed we wouldn't," Louise answered quickly.

Her pulse had quickened. Was she going to get a clue to the strange situation in the little town?

Before telling his story, Mr. Murphy suggested that his daughter go upstairs and change her clothes. After she was gone, he leaned toward the Danas. "What I'm about to tell you is not for a child's ears. I strongly suspect that some of the town officials are in league with outsiders of ill repute.

What they're up to, I don't know, but I'm sure it is underhanded."

"I suppose," Louise said, "you wouldn't care to mention any names?"

Mr. Murphy shook his head. "I live here with my wife and child. I wouldn't want them to be harmed."

Jean agreed. "To tell the truth, my sister and I have wondered what the motives are behind the sabotage."

Louise asked Mr. Murphy if he knew that employees at the inn had received threatening letters and left.

"No, I didn't," he answered. "I'm sorry to hear that."

By this time Mary was on her way downstairs and the talk ceased. The Danas stood up and said they must leave. Mr. Murphy thanked them again for saving his little girl and hoped he would see them before they returned home.

Mary shyly said good-by to them and added, "You're awfully nice people."

The Danas waved and drove off toward the inn. Conversation reverted to the carpenter. Except for his evident trust in Mr. Uhler, his suspicions and theirs about Horizon coincided.

"I'm convinced," Jean declared, "that we'll find answers to this mystery in the vicinity of the old lighthouse!"

When the girls arrived at the inn, they changed

their clothes. At the desk Jean learned Ken and Chris were to be in a surfing contest that afternoon.

"Let's ask Doris and Evelyn to go down to the beach with us," Louise proposed.

"Good idea."

Their two friends were eager to share the adventure. "I suppose," Evelyn remarked, "the phantom surfer won't be around. But we can help you hunt for clues at the promontory."

When Ken and Chris heard what the four girls intended to do, they made them promise not to go inside the lighthouse.

As the Starhurst classmates approached the area, Doris commented, "No one seems to be around. What do you think we should look for?"

"Anything that might have been dropped which is connected with money or surfing," Louise replied.

At Jean's suggestion to separate, each girl took a different direction. Louise's steps led her near the secret entrance in the large sand dune. Though the sun's glare was blinding, the young detective was sure she detected a rim of light around the door.

"Someone's inside!" she told herself, hurrying forward.

The brush which covered it had been tumbled aside and the padlock was unfastened. Louise inched closer, hugging the edge of the dune.

When she reached the door, Louise could distinctly hear voices inside. Sentences were muffled,

"Someone's inside!" Louise told herself

but she heard isolated words—"phantom," "to-night," "wad," "finish."

By this time Louise's mind was in a whirl. "Wad means money," she thought. "Could this mean counterfeit money?"

She figured that "phantom" and "tonight" meant the phantom would appear that night. But "finish" puzzled her. Did it mean the whole scheme was finished? Or had the batch of counterfeit money been "finished"?

Suddenly a voice above her roared, "What do you think you're doing?"

Louise looked up to the top of the dune. The man was one of the lumber thieves! Would he kidnap and imprison her inside the dune?

Louise stammered an answer to his question. "I—I came over here with friends for a walk. We got separated. They're not here so I'll look for them somewhere else."

She was sure that he had not recognized her. He growled, "This is private property. It is a dangerous place. Get out and stay out!"

Louise pretended to be only too glad to go and scurried off. She found her friends some distance away and told them what had happened.

"I feel it's too dangerous for us to stay around here," Doris said fearfully. "Louise, don't you think you should report this to the State Police?"

"By the time they could get here," Louise responded, "the men would be gone."

"That's right," Jean agreed. "And besides, we'd better wait until we have something more concrete than a disconnected conversation to report."

As the girls approached the beach of the Horizon Inn, they were greeted by their dates. At once Ken said, "Chris won the contest! He didn't wipe out once!"

"Wonderful!" Jean cried.

Chris grinned, then asked what the girls had found out. The boys were amazed at their adventures.

Ken spoke up. "This means, of course, that you Danas will invite Chris and me to accompany you to the lighthouse tonight."

"Correct," Louise replied, chuckling. She turned to Evelyn's date. "Please don't tell anyone about our plans." He promised not to.

When the Danas reached their room, Louise telephoned State Police Headquarters. She reported that the girls had seen one of the lumber thieves on the dunes outside of Horizon.

Sergeant Wilk thanked her and said an investigation would be made.

Late that evening the Danas and their dates left the inn. Louise was carrying a large flashlight and Ken had the spyglass. The couples took the circuitous route across the dunes to the lighthouse. As the girls passed the secret door, they saw light peeking through.

The group crouched on the sand and watched

both the lighthouse and the ocean. For over an hour nothing happened.

"The ship's never come at the same time," Jean put in. As she spoke, the mysterious yacht suddenly hove into view. It stopped but did not turn off its lights.

Louise looked through the spyglass. "Somebody's climbing down the outside ladder," she reported. "But it's too dark at the water line for me to see what he's doing."

"Maybe he's coming ashore in a rowboat," Ken said.

Chris suggested he might even be the phantom surfer.

He had barely said this when Jean whispered, "Up in the tower! Someone is signaling with a light!"

The onlookers surmised that the beam was guiding the man toward shore.

"Ken and Chris," said Jean, "why don't you go up into the tower and nab that guy? Louise and I will stay down here and watch for the phantom surfer!"

CHAPTER XVIII

An Accusation

MINUTES after Ken and Chris had left the girls, the moon came out brightly. The Danas could see the shimmering ocean clearly.

"Louise," said Jean ten minutes later, "the light in the tower has gone out!"

"I wonder if the boys captured the signaler," her sister said.

They watched the door of the lighthouse and hoped to see it open.

"I wish we could go up there and find out what's happening!" Jean was impatient.

At that instant the door opened. A man rushed out and started for the dunes. Close behind him were Ken and Chris running at top speed. Suddenly they paused as if unsure which way to go.

"To your right!" Jean shouted at the top of her voice.

Ken waved and the boys vanished from sight.

The girls turned their attention back to the pounding surf.

Presently Jean grabbed Louise's arm. "I think I see the phantom surfer coming!"

The white-clad figure was climbing and dropping rhythmically on the face of a giant wave.

"We must try to see him closer," Louise said, and dashed forward over the sand. Reaching the edge of the water, she trained her flashlight beam full on the surfer. The girls stared almost speechless.

"Bing!" they exclaimed together.

The next moment the wave formed a great canopy. It dropped with flying spray like an enormous curtain.

Bing had vanished!

"Where is he?" Louise asked fearfully.

Jean suggested that when the surfer saw the flashlight he had disappeared deliberately. When they failed to sight him again, the girls thought that perhaps the phantom surfer had made his way to the tunnel in the promontory.

"He'll probably come up out of that trap door," Jean said. "Let's go inside the lighthouse and surprise him."

"All right," Louise agreed.

They hurried across the beach, wondering what Bing would tell them. Was he just night surfing for fun? Or was he connected in some way with the ship, the signaling, and even the counterfeit money?

"I just can't believe he's leading a double life," Jean remarked.

They entered the lighthouse and waited. Five minutes went by. Ten. Fifteen!

"I guess he isn't going to come up here after all," Louise said, disappointed.

The girls went outdoors again. Ken and Chris were just returning from the chase across the dunes.

"Did you catch the signaler in the tower?" Jean asked.

Chris shook his head. "He literally evaporated. Guess he knows these dunes so well it was easy for him to hide."

"Do you suppose he might be behind the secret door in the large dune?" Jean asked. She started running toward it.

The padlock was intact, indicating one thing to the foursome. If the man had been there at all, it was only for a short time. He probably had ducked out and locked the hideout while the girls were inside the lighthouse.

"Jean, if you're right, then a lot of things would begin to make sense. The signaling between the tower and yacht and the counterfeiting activity would be definitely linked!" her sister declared.

Louise also told the boys that they had had a good look at the phantom surfer and were sure he was Bing Master. The announcement fell like a bombshell.

Ken asked, "Where do you think our friend

went?" Before the others could say anything, he answered his own question. "Maybe Bing's hiding in that tunnel!"

Louise smiled. "I'd say we're on the same wave length. Let's find out."

The two couples rushed into the old building and lifted the trap door.

"I'd like to go down and take a look," Louise said.

"Okay," Ken agreed, "but follow me."

He descended the iron rungs, beaming his strong flashlight into the inky blackness. Louise focused hers into the shallow depths.

"You stay at the foot of the ladder a moment," Ken directed. "I'll wade out and see if I can find Bing."

As Louise stood on the bottom rung she flashed her light around the interior of the rocky cavern. Presently the beams picked up a hook wedged among the rocks. Hanging from it just out of her reach was an apparently waterproof sack, whose brown color camouflaged its presence.

"Ken!" she called out. "I've found something! How about you?"

There was no answer but within a few seconds she spotted Ken. He reported that the phantom surfer was not hiding in the tunnel.

"I hope nothing happened to him!" Louise said worriedly.

"I'd say he has a lot of explaining to do," Ken remarked.

Louise pointed to the sack hanging on the rocky wall. "Don't you think we should examine it?" she asked.

"Yes, I do. We'll carry it upstairs and take a look." He unhooked the sack.

Jean and Chris were amazed at the find. Quickly they opened the bag and pulled out a package exactly like the one that had been found along the dunes. Though they were suspicious of the contents, no one said a word. The string was untied and the paper pulled off.

"More counterfeit money I'll bet!" Chris exclaimed. "I'll count it."

Quickly he riffled the bills. Again there was five thousand dollars.

"Those counterfeiters don't fool around," Ken commented. "Well, shall we take the package with us and put it in Mr. Olney's safe?"

Jean grinned. "It really doesn't need that much protection. I think Louise and I can keep it in our room. I doubt that anyone will come to retrieve it."

Ken did not completely agree. "That's true, but these are hot bills and valuable evidence. The counterfeiter will want to get them back to protect himself."

He insisted upon taking the money and delivering it to the State Police Headquarters the following day.

On the way back to the inn, Louise asked if the boys could describe the man who had fled from the tower. They had not seen his face, but both said he was rather tall.

"I'll bet," Louise remarked, "that he was either Mack or Mike. We don't know which is the tall one and which is the short one."

Ken said there was no logic in the men carrying on small-time thievery if they were part of a counterfeit racket. "I'm sure that stolen lumber would bring them very little profit," he added.

"That's true," she agreed. "I doubt that their primary purpose is to make a profit on the thefts, but the lumber and supply raids have delayed the restoration project considerably. You can all fill in from there."

"Pretty cagey," Chris spoke up. "Keep the visitors away to let the counterfeiters play!"

"There are plenty of other things, though, that I can't fathom," Louise added. "For one thing that secret door into the sand dune. I wonder if perhaps there's a printing press inside. When the bills are ready, they're packed into the waterproof bags and taken to the mysterious ship. Then they're distributed to foreign countries."

Jean and the boys agreed this was a possibility. Was the phantom surfer the relay from the tunnel to the yacht?

"But if so," Jean objected, "why did Bing leave the sack there tonight?"

Chris suggested that maybe the surfer had been injured when he had suddenly disappeared under the giant wave and was unable to carry out his errand. The thought of his being hurt sobered the group. Though they all felt he was mixed up in the mystery, they shuddered to think of his being injured or perhaps dead!

To their complete amazement when they arrived at the inn, they saw Bing dancing with Doris! The Danas and their dates looked at one another in disbelief. How in the world had he slipped back from the lighthouse without being seen?

In a short time the band played the closing number. The Danas had already gone to their room and in a few minutes Doris and Evelyn came to knock on their door.

"How did you make out?" Evelyn asked at once.

"We had a terribly exciting time," Louise replied. "Before I tell you what happened, I want to know about your evening. Doris, was Bing with you the whole time?"

"No, he wasn't. He received a phone call, excused himself, and went off for about an hour. Why?"

Louise and Jean now told their story. When they announced that Bing was the phantom surfer, Doris cried out, "Oh no!"

Louise went on to reveal her discovery of the second package of counterfeit money.

"Doris, it begins to look," Jean said, "as if Bing

is part of a racket. We haven't figured it all out, but the ship and someone in the tower were signaling lights to each other. The counterfeit money and Bing taking his life in his hands by surfing toward the rocks indicate a pretty nefarious business."

Doris had sat down on one of the beds. All the color had drained from her face. "I can't believe it," she said with a catch in her voice. "I just can't believe it."

Louise put an arm around the girl. "Doris, I'm terribly sorry, but for your own protection you'll have to stop dating Bing. If you don't, the police might think you were an accomplice."

This was too much for Doris. She burst into tears and flung herself face down on the bed. The other girls were not sure how to comfort her and sat in silence for several seconds.

Finally the sad-eyed girl stood up and turned to the sisters defiantly. "You don't know Bing as well as I do," Doris said, her jaw set firmly. "He's not dishonest, I'm sure of that. He's a wonderful person, and I don't think it's fair of you to accuse him of something crooked!"

She went on to say that Jean and Louise were just weaving a story and had only circumstantial evidence to go on.

"I will admit there's a mystery in Horizon and it probably has to do with the counterfeit money," Doris said, "but I'm positive Bing isn't doing anything wrong. He has a right to be heard before being condemned, so he can clear himself."

"You're absolutely right," Louise agreed. "I'll tell you what. Why don't we call his room right now and ask him to meet us in the beach house in ten minutes? I'll call Ken and Chris, too, and tell them to bring that package of counterfeit bills."

Doris looked relieved and waited while Louise phoned the three young men. All agreed to meet at the beach house where they would not be disturbed. Other guests at the inn had been conscientiously obeying the sign of not venturing onto the beach after dark. The notice had been left hanging in the lobby as more of a protection than a warning.

The Starhurst group and their dates had assembled before Bing appeared. He seemed as jaunty as ever. Getting no response to his levity, he asked, "Why are you all so solemn? Is this an initiation of some sort?"

"Oh, Bing," Doris cried out, "you're—you're not a crook, are you?"

The surfer laughed. "My word, no. Where did you get that idea?"

Louise now held up the bag of counterfeit money which Ken had given her to put into her beach bag.

Facing Bing, she asked, "How do you explain the five thousand dollars of phony bills?"

CHAPTER XIX

Planning an Attack

BING MASTER stared at the bulky bag in utter astonishment. Then he searched the faces of the young people.

"Where did you get this?" he demanded.

Jean answered, "In the lighthouse tunnel—after you perhaps hung it there."

Louise added, "This is the second package of counterfeit money we've found."

"Where did you find the other one?" Bing queried.

"On the sand dunes."

Bing requested that the Danas and their friends reveal everything they knew.

Louise shook her head. "Not until you tell us who you really are and how you are involved in the counterfeit ring."

The young man blinked. "Why are you deliberately setting traps for me? How do you expect me to reveal any secrets to you until you tell me what *you* know?" The boys and girls looked at one another and gave silent consent to Bing's request.

Louise said, "In case you're wondering why we're eager to solve the mystery, Mr. Olney can answer that. He has asked Jean and me to trace the source of warning letters that were sent to members of his staff and frightened them so much most of them walked out."

Bing said, of course, he was aware of this, but he had no idea who was behind the threats. "I'm not even sure it has anything to do with the mystery of the counterfeit money."

Jean spoke up. "We are. There are certain townspeople we strongly suspect of being connected with the sabotaging of the restoration project. No doubt they're also responsible for the petty thievery and probably the counterfeiting."

Ken added, "They don't want visitors so they're making it difficult for the inn to stay open."

Bing's look of shock had not left his face. "You all amaze me. I had no idea you were sleuthing. Of course I saw you poking around the lighthouse, but I thought you were just exploring for fun." He smiled. "Well, since you know so much about the whole thing, I will tell you something in confidence. Do I have your promise that you won't discuss it with anyone?"

His listeners nodded and eagerly waited for him to continue. His announcement stunned them.

"I am a secret agent of the United States Treasury Department."

To prove this, Bing opened his coat and showed his identification.

Doris was the first to recover from the surprise. "Oh, Bing, I knew all along you were fine and honest!" He smiled at her appreciatively.

Louise spoke up. "Bing, I think we all owe you an apology. Of course we're very curious to know what your part is in the case, but perhaps you're not permitted to tell us."

He gave a boyish grin. "There's no harm in confirming that what you already know is true."

He revealed that he and other agents had been working on the case for over a month.

"It's a very puzzling one," he said. "Unlike most counterfeiting operations, the money is not printed in this country but on one of the Caribbean Islands."

"And you haven't stopped the racket?" Evelyn asked Bing.

"No," he replied. "We are trying to locate the top man in this country who receives and distributes the bills. After all, we have no jurisdiction over the island."

Bing told his young listeners since he was an expert swimmer and surfer he had been asked to try making contact with a yacht which the department suspected was bringing the money to the United States.

"One day, while the ship was anchored beyond the lighthouse, I swam out to it. Pretending to be exhausted, I cried for help. The crew took me aboard.

"Again I played a part. I posed as a disgruntled citizen while trying to find out something about the ship and its operation. At last I learned that a man went over the side and rowed to shore with the packages of counterfeit money. But in the rough waves around the lighthouse area, he nearly lost his life several times and some of the packages were washed overboard.

"Finally I offered my services, saying I would be glad to swim out and meet the rowboat. After a lot of consultation, the captain agreed to this arrangement and said he would pay me well. Of course he didn't tell me it would be counterfeit money."

Bing laughed softly. "That was very clever of him. He figured if I were caught with the money, it would look bad for me and the authorities wouldn't believe my story. I asked him where he wanted the money delivered and he told me about the old pirates' tunnel leading to the lighthouse. I was to hang the bags in there."

He explained that he had attached each one to the back of his wet suit's belt.

Jean asked, "Why did you wear a white suit and cap and let people think you were a phantom surfer?"

The secret agent said that the water cooled off at night and it would be impossible for him to stay in it for the length of time required without a thermal rubber suit.

"You probably wonder why you never saw me on the beach after I had been in the tunnel. I swam back to the beach house and changed my clothes there."

Bing revealed that at various times when the yacht appeared, other secret agents had posted themselves near the lighthouse and even inside it. They knew about the trap door to the tunnel. Each time after waiting in vain for a counterfeiter to appear, they would open it to surprise him. But to their dismay someone had already picked up the counterfeit money and disappeared before he could be caught. The question was, Where had he gone?

Louise asked Bing if he knew about the door in the dune. He replied No.

"The entrance is well camouflaged," Louise said, and told how her group had discovered it.

Jean spoke up. "You know what I think? Maybe there's an underground passage that leads from the tunnel to that sand dune."

The agent nodded, then requested the Danas to tell him their suspicions about the townspeople's possible involvement in the counterfeit scheme.

"We think the sabotage is a cover-up," Louise answered. "We suspect the mayor, the constable, and probably Mr. Uhler, the contractor. They pretend to be country bumpkins but are probably about as clever and dishonest as men can be."

Chris spoke up. "Bing, when is your next assignment?"

"Tomorrow night."

At once the Danas offered to help the agent solve the mystery. Doris and the boys insisted upon going with them.

Bing frowned. "I couldn't let you take such dangerous risks. I'm sure that the men involved in the counterfeit ring are getting worried about your astuteness and may pull out. Louise, perhaps the word 'finish' you heard at the dune means that tomorrow night will be the end of their activity in this area."

"Then that's all the more reason why we should help you," Louise urged. "Couldn't we be posted at different places? We could carry whistles to summon one another in case of trouble."

Bing smiled. With a sigh he said, "I have no right to give you any such permission, but if you just happen to be in the vicinity, well—"

The young people laughed and said they could hardly wait for action. Bing told them he would alert his coagents to expect to see three girls and two young men sneaking around the beach and the sand dunes.

"Our agents will cover the lighthouse," he said.

"I'll go through my usual performance as a phantom surfer so none of my contacts will become suspicious."

He added, "Tomorrow I plan to put on a surfing show for the benefit of all the house-party groups. I realize you'll be going home soon."

Before the young people said good night, they turned over the sack of counterfeit money to Bing.

The agent nodded appreciatively. "Good work, kids," he said.

Next morning after a hearty Sunday brunch, the three couples attended church in Lawrenceville. Shortly after their return, they donned swimsuits and went to the beach. The Danas noticed that Lettie and her group were absent and inquired about them. They were told that Mrs. Briggs had checked out.

Jean grinned. Then she puckered her lips and her eyes twinkled as she said, "What a shame! Just think what Lettie's going to miss!"

Bing began his show with some hot dogging. He chose a special surfboard—one that was short and maneuverable. As he waded into the water he turned, waved, and called out, "Cowabunga!"

As he rode in, there were gasps of admiration and applause for Bing's fast turns, tricky footwork, fancy stances, and pull-outs while still maintaining perfect balance on the board.

Before going out again, Bing announced, "Now I'll do an *el spontaneo*."

His excited audience watched in amazement as their instructor rode in with his head between his knees and his arms wrapped around them. The applause was thunderous. He acknowledged it modestly with a big grin.

"One more performance," Bing told the spectators. "Then you take to the boards. This next one is called a flying swan."

Bing looked among the crowd and called out, "Doris, where are you?"

Doris Harland arose and walked to his side. He smiled and said, "This is my partner for the flying swan."

Even the Danas were astounded that Doris had lost all fear of surfing. Under Bing's teaching, she apparently had become excellent at the sport. They began to clap loudly as she and Bing, who had propped a large foamie on his head, waded into the surf.

A few minutes later they were out far enough to start the performance. The attractive couple climbed onto the extra-long board. Then, to everyone's amazement, Bing hoisted Doris to his shoulders and held her ankles. The ride started.

"They're sure giving it their all," said Ken.

The tandem ride was perfectly executed. Doris had never seemed happier and the ovation she and her partner received was overwhelming.

Blushing, Doris said, "Bing is the most terrific surfing teacher in the world!"

Louise and Jean were thinking, "And one of the most terrific secret agents!"

That evening they set off for the lighthouse area with Ken, Chris, and Doris. When the couples separated, Doris remained with Jean and Chris.

Louise and Ken chose a spot to hide near the secret door and squatted down in the sand to await developments. There was no conversation for fear of their being detected. Both kept their eyes on the ocean, watching for the appearance of the phantom surfer.

They had been waiting about ten minutes when the door in the dune opened. As the couple jumped up, huge hands were clamped over their mouths. They were dragged inside the dark sand dune.

Both of them fought like tigers, but they were outnumbered. Louise and Ken lost the battle. Bound and gagged, they were thrust onto the damp floor.

A deep voice said, "Now we'll get the rest of the kids!"

CHAPTER XX

Pirates' Passageway

It was pitch black inside the dune. Louise and Ken could not see who their captors were.

The men began to argue on how to capture "the rest of the kids" without taking the chance of being caught themselves.

One said, "The outside door isn't a secret any more. We'd better leave here and fasten the padlock on it so nobody will be able to get to these two."

"What'll we do with the cash that's in here?" another asked. "I'm not going without it."

"You're nuts!" a third man said. "You want to get picked up with hot money?"

A fourth companion suggested that they stay right where they were and lay low. "What are you all so scared about?" he queried. "Everything's arranged with the surfer and he's never let us down yet."

The argument continued. Louise and Ken did not recognize any of the voices. The couple stopped struggling, fascinated by what they were hearing.

"Pretty soon you'll start being suspicious of the mayor and the constable," the man said. He laughed sardonically. "If it hadn't been for them, treasury agents would have been onto us by now."

Another man laughed softly. "But Ritter and Canby weren't able to get rid of those kids that have been snooping around here and in town. I wish that one of those bombs Mack set at the old house had blown up the whole bunch!"

"Well, we've got two of them. Come on! We'd better get the others right now!"

At his insistence, the four men went out the secret door. Louise and Ken could hear the padlock being put into place.

Once more the couple started struggling to free themselves. They tried rolling on the ground to loosen the gags and bonds but their captors had done a good job.

Suddenly they heard indistinct voices which seemed to come from below them. One said, "I ain't done nuthin' wrong. The lighthouse was dangerous for strangers to be in. When those kids came around, I hid in the tunnel and made wailin' sounds to scare 'em off."

"We think you did more than that, Slick. You're an old-timer at counterfeiting. Didn't you drop a packet of money on the dunes?" The questioner was Bing!

"My pal did," Slick replied. "You can't prove I knew what was in the package. I was just a messenger."

Without warning, the floor beneath Louise began to move upward. She was rolled to one side.

Instantly the place was filled with bright light. Bing Master appeared from below through a trap door, urging his prisoner in front of him. Slick was carrying a waterproof bag, which no doubt contained counterfeit money.

Bing saw Louise and Ken lying on the floor, bound and gagged. While keeping a wary eye on Slick, he quickly released them.

"Oh, thank you!" Louise exclaimed.

"What a relief!" Ken added, and told what had happened. "Our captors left and locked the door." Then he asked, "How did you get here?"

Bing explained that he had decided to remain in darkness in the tunnel after hanging up the waterproof bag. As Jean had predicted, there was a concealed entrance from the tunnel to a brick-lined passageway. This in turn led to the dune. It was part of an old hiding place built by pirates. The door had been put in more recently.

Bing went on, "When a section of wall opened and Slick came out and took the bag, I closed in."

While investigating the room under the sand

dune, the sleuths discovered several piles of packaged counterfeit money. With Ken's help, Bing had already gagged and bound his prisoner.

"We'll come back for him later," he said. "Right now we'd better get outside and see what's going on."

The three went down an iron ladder and through the brick passage which had a ceiling so low they had to stoop. When they reached the watery tunnel, the secret agent and the two amateur detectives climbed the rusty rungs leading to the lighthouse. Ken raised the trap door and the trio hurried out to the beach.

The bright moonlight revealed a scene of wild excitement. Jean, Doris, and Chris had spotted a man sneaking through the dunes and had overtaken him. Now they were holding onto the struggling figure. Running toward the group were two men whom Bing identified to his friends as agents. Within seconds the agents clamped handcuffs on the young people's captive.

Jean spoke up excitedly, "This is the man who made the threat on the telephone! I recognize his voice."

"You mean the one who frightened away the waitresses and chambermaids and porters?" Louise asked.

"Yes. Now Mr. Olney can get them back!"

"And the restoration can be put in the hands of a reliable contractor," Louise said.

The man scowled at the girl. "You kids know too much," he said.

Louise replied, "I suppose you left the threatening letters for the girls and the porters. Were they written on board that yacht?"

The prisoner jumped as if astounded that she had hit upon the truth. "Yes, I did, but I had a right to do it. Me and my friends didn't want a lot of people at that inn, especially snoopers like you. I put a sign up in the lobby to keep everybody away from the beach at night."

Jean said, "We don't scare easy."

Within minutes more agents were arriving with others they had taken into custody. One was the man who had done the signaling from the tower.

It was revealed that the counterfeiting gang had devised their own code. The first time the girls had seen the swinging light it had meant that there would be no pickup of the fake money that evening. The second message was just the reverse: the men on board were to send in the largest amount which the phantom surfer could carry.

As the Danas and their friends were listening to confessions, they noticed two handcuffed men being led up the beach by other agents.

"Constable Ritter and Mayor Canby!" Jean burst out.

The two were protesting wildly that they knew nothing about the counterfeit ring and the saboteurs and thieves in Horizon. Quickly Louise whispered to Bing what her four captors had been discussing inside the sand dune. He confronted the pair with this information.

Once more they denied the accusation, but in a few minutes the other four men were rounded up. All of them accused Ritter and Canby of masterminding the whole project.

"That contractor Uhler is also implicated," one of the agents told Bing. "There's a warrant out now for his arrest. State Police have already arrested his two workmen Mike and Mack."

The T-man had other news too. The captain and crew of the yacht, and the man in the rowboat, had been taken into custody and government officials on the Caribbean Islands had been asked to round up the printers of the counterfeit money.

"I guess that just about winds up everything!" Bing remarked to the other agents. "And now I want to introduce you all to Louise and Jean Dana and their friends Doris Harland, Ken Scott, and Chris Barton. They're a great bunch of surfers and sleuths. Just look how speedily they wiped out the mystery of Horizon!"

The agents gave a cheer, but their prisoners glared in hate at the young people. Louise and Jean were accustomed to this reaction of captured criminals. But it never stopped the girls from finding mysteries and wanting to solve them.

Bing went on, "Before my new friends return to school, I'm going to give a big party for them."

Jean asked with a twinkle in her eye, "In the surf or out of it?"

"It'll be a combination," the secret agent replied. "First we'll do some hot dogging on the surfboards and then we'll have a beach picnic."

"Cool!" Chris called out.

Louise whispered to Ken, "I think we should leave. These men have work to do." She said to Bing, "We're going back to the inn now. See you later."

The agents said good-by to the girls and their friends, then the young people slowly walked up the beach. Ken and Chris congratulated the Danas for adding another gold medal to their long list of successful cases.

Louise smiled, "I think this time the gold medal goes to Doris. She never once doubted the phantom surfer!"